UNDERGROUND

MAYHEM

GK JURRENS

eBook ISBN: 978-1-952165–07-8
Print ISBN: 978-1-952165-04-7
v.220706_0733

GKJurrens.com

DEDICATION

This book is dedicated to an amazing young lady who has inspired millions worldwide, including yours truly. She possesses the courage so many of us lack. Sixteen-year-old Greta Thunberg's superpower —autism—enables clarity of thought and vision to which we can all aspire, *if we choose.*
In particular, her "How Dare You!" speech to the 2019 United Nations Climate Action Summit seized this septuagenarian's heart and mind! She also reminds us that *different* can be really bad *or* good.
Thank you, Greta! I can't wait to witness your next episode.

And to a young man not much older than Greta who treasures his anonymity, who shares Greta's super-power, and who seems inspired to pluck greatness from the doldrums of his everyday life. You will do great things... great things... if only you dare to dream. - GK

DISCLAIMER

ACKNOWLEDGMENTS

- Thanks and apologies to my long-suffering wife, Kay, to all of my beta readers (Judy Rineheimer, Julia Stocksdale, Judy Howard...), and *especially* to _all_ you dear readers.
- And to Nick Russell, New York Times best-selling author.

So I will see each of you on the road or in *The Alley*.

Subscribe at GKJurrens.com

Whether you read all or a portion of this book, please consider emailing the author a brief review of your impressions at gjurrens@yahoo.com

Or post an honest review wherever this book is offered at online retail stores and reader sites like Goodreads.

Thanks in advance.

- GK

INTRODUCTION

Welcome to *Underground,* book one of the *Mayhem* trilogy.

At the end of each of my books, I've included useful reference material:

- The **cast of major characters** and their respective roles are listed for you (Appendix A),
- **A visual *map* lays out relationships** between all major characters within and across story lines (Appendix B),
- **A glossary of terms** commonly used in the twenty-second century. Like you, many of these terms were new to me (Appendix C).

Alternatively, you might find the trilogy's companion guide useful (sold separately under the title of ***The Glimpse)***. This brief book contains all the information above for the entire trilogy along with additional content for this time in future history. Some readers use this as a resource while reading the Mayhem series.

Enjoy what I hope will be a fun and thought-provoking read.

- GK

PREFACE

Isaiah French, a.k.a. Zaya, started publishing episodes of the *Redemption Alley* journal as a lark, hawking his research skills as they collided with his inquisitive nature and propensity to show off. He uncovered new and shocking information, digging out facts under the guise that they were for entertainment purposes only—a frail safety net, at best. Not much, but that ploy kept him out of jail. So far. Zaya moved too fast to worry about time-consuming journalistic *trivigalities*—trivial legalities—such as two confirmations for each factoid, or to abide by sundry *morethics* (moral and ethical rules). These shortcuts have earned him more than a few scars, and not just professionally.

Some have said he's a bulldog, because he'd chew on a story, even old dried-out bones—if it intrigues him—no matter how long it takes or how scarce the bits of meat that are left on the bone, or how financially destitute his debtors claim he's become. Zaya would say, "Just malicious rumors. The universe always provides."

1

———————

Express Skyway
Outside
New Wash,
Maryginia
June 2150

ZAYA STOOD READY TO DIE TONIGHT IF NEED BE, ALTHOUGH HE hoped that wouldn't be necessary. He thought, *If they catch me, if my hair-brained plan fails, I'm dead.* That would spell disaster—not just for him, for everyone. *Well, I've already lived longer than I ever expected. The least of my worries.*

He could grow just as passionate about a spirited street scrap as much as drawing bad people out of the shadows and digging out their secrets. His passion was his secret weapon. But now they knew that too.

Every one of Zaya's scars told its own story, and he had earned many. Even though he avoided fights, they did not avoid him. He suspected that at some point someone had embedded a trouble-locator chip under his skin and wired it to his brain—Zaya never backed away from a fight or from a story. Constitutionally, he was incapable of accepting defeat. He could not explain it, nor would he try.

His house—his home—screamed down the skyway at a hundred knots as it sliced through a late Spring drizzle, commanding just a meter of altitude above the plasticrete slab. Reflections from his road beams hinted of its pitted surface. The ride roughened with every additional knot. Zaya's white pony tail shimmered with the excessive vibration until it disappeared, wedged between the middle of his back and the once-creamy, now-cracked contraband leather seat.

As he tweaked the old transport's controls for the sixth time in as many seconds, Zaya mumbled, *In the eight years you've owned me, you beast, I've never pushed you past seventy-five knots, or above ten meters. Oh well. You'll always give me a little more. You'd better.* But then he softened his internal monologue just in case the old bus was, what, listening? Getting her feelings hurt? *Good grief. What the Hell am I thinking?*

He had already coerced the eighteen-year-old bus twenty knots past her theoretical maximum hull speed as he rocketed her forty-tons through the hazy darkness. A sweeping network of spider-lace lightning flashed across the oxygen-deprived sky just ahead. Not enough air for thunder. Now and then, that blue sky fire dimly illuminated the all but deserted thoroughfare.

Eight thrusters, one nestled just inboard of each tire shield, canted their business ends fifty degrees aft to demand beyond-reckless levels of horizontal thrust. That meant less vertical thrust. If Zaya pitched them any farther aft, the entire rig would drop like a lead ingot. But what choice did he have, mere seconds ahead of a horrible death? He needed to control their precise point of confrontation.

Sparse commercial traffic dominated the New Wash-Philly skyway this late at night, all ponderous by comparison to him and his pursuers streaking past. Truck drivers never slept, it seemed, although most rigs required no drivers. But those that did, never drove this low or this fast. The periodic red lane lights atop sensors embedded in the magnetically-repelled roadway offered subtle night-vision guidance for those stupid enough to drive in manual mode. Zaya's bus ripped over the red sensors so fast and so close they appeared as near-invisible solid lines. But this low, and at this speed, the bus would have been quick to respond to those sensors' emitters, had he allowed that. Zaya grumbled to himself, *Not this fool. Not in this bus. Not this night.*

A hasty glance confirmed his fears. All the mirrors and cams confirmed they had closed the gap. His pursuers knew him to be a dangerous thief. Of secrets. A whistleblower. But worse than his own demise, if he didn't outlive these hired thugs, a story of heinous malevolence on a monumental scale would go untold and unchecked. The legislation sure to follow his demise, his story untold, would legitimize alliance-sponsored mass murder by time-elapsed assassination.

He had *so* many questions!

Zaya felt invincible. Mostly. But even with his potent physique, no matter how buff, *nobody* survived a direct hit from a pulser. He slammed the heel of his left hand on the dash and grimaced at the pain. *God, I hate those things. Like outrunning death by toaster.*

. . .

THE BUS WAS OLD BUT CAPABLE. HIS ANCIENT TRANSPORT PRE-dated pulse weapon technology by at least a decade. While the bombardment excited the molecules of his bus's shiny fuselage, trying to fry its ancient systems, the barrage did nothing to disable his flight controls or drive-train. He swiped at the sweat running in rivulets down his temples and checked the gauges. *Getting warm in here. Gotta do something before I'm roasted.* Zaya smirked at his foolhardiness. *Manual control at this speed and just a meter above certain death? Ha!*

But he needed everything his old transport could deliver, and he knew her better than his old auto-fly *cruise* system ever would. Besides, the little extra lift from the ground's proximity gave him a boost, albeit a small one. Despite the risk, he put even more forward pressure on the stick. As he gripped it with white knuckles, he resisted the forces applied by turbulent side winds generated by a sudden drop in barometric pressure. That seemed to happen a lot these days. Those lateral forces tried to whip his twenty-five meter articulated rig sideways from the skyway. *Yet one more reason manual control is a stupid idea!* With little choice, he kicked in a touch of linear stabilizer to negate the transverse forces, though that would cost him a knot or two. That fancy crap seldom worked anymore, but the old bus surprised him again. Tonight it worked.

THE GAGGLE OF GOONS GOT CLOSER. ZAYA CURSED THAT FLAT-black Trans-Sport as it further narrowed the gap. *Geez, that thing is fast! This is not going according to plan!* As he edged the stick even farther forward, he pushed it a millimeter too far. Typical. The transport's alumasteel nose bounced off the roadway with bone-shattering finality. His forward momentum had overwhelmed the skyway's far weaker mag-lev field below. Magnetic levitation was never designed to overcome so much horizontal thrust and so little vertical.

That's when he heard the voice coming from within. *"The ditch is your salvation, Zaya. Use it! Now!"*

As he lost vertical thrust trying for more forward speed, the nose of his forty-ton transport kissed the edge of the plasticrete roadway a second time. He obeyed the voice, slammed the stick to his right. That command granted him a few meters of grace. The forward skid plates under his fuselage dug into soft earth of the broad emergency ditch as wide as a barren field. Far better than auguring into the unforgiving slab. Another chance to live a while longer.

Time for a new tactic, cowboy. Zaya eased back on the violently vibrating stick and returned it to amidships. The fuselage regained an uneasy course a few meters up, at least less ground turbulence farther from the ground, but now he hurtled toward a galaxy of lights twinkling in the hazy atmosphere. If he maintained course and altitude, hundreds would die. But stopping in time wasn't possible. If he climbed in the bus's current state, any failure would plummet him to certain death. *Well, an easy choice. Let's do it, old gal.*

He jerked back on the stick and jammed both feet to the floorboard, dumping raw pressurized hydrogen into all eight thrusters now swiveled the nose to near *Full Vertical.*

The ponderous bus shot up faster than its design should have allowed, and just nimble enough to clear the sixty-floor housing complex on the far side of the dusty field. His pursuers kept pace.

*"Head for the flood tunnels that run parallel to the skyway, just on the far side of these apartment buildings. Turn left. **Now.**"*

He trusted the voice that already saved his life once tonight. No, he trusted *her,* although he acknowledged fear of capture, torture, or death more easily than the widening gap in his emotional armor. *She makes my stomach flutter.* He smiled. *Aw, what the Hell. No way I'll outlive her anyway.*

Zaya jammed the stick forward. At the same time, he stomped more pressure onto the pedal under his right foot, less on the left, stick to the left. The bus obediently dived hard and skewed left with that cross-control maneuver. A tunnel entrance appeared as if by magic in front of him. Black on black. No lights. Illuminated only by occasional sky fire. The oval maw looked to be about twice as wide and high as his transport, but he understood why she suggested the tunnel. Precision driving—his specialty.

*Let's see if those assholes can do **this**....* Zaya brought the stick to its center detente and eased up just a little on both thruster pedals. At the same instant he nudged the stick forward, using his starboard thrusters and his trim's fine-tuning controls on the dash to tweak his course without banking. His stomach churned. He ignored the clammy goo in his throat. *Hang onto your clenched glutes, you idiot.*

Was this tunnel long and straight? No telling. Neither would it give him any visual frame of reference once it consumed him and his bus, but he gambled he had flyway. He throttled back, but only to sixty knots, punched in *cruise. Can't steer if I can't see. Thank God cruise doesn't need satellites. Hope this proximity shit still works.*

As he wished good karma on the old bus's control and propulsion systems, he touched another button on the cockpit's dash screen to lower the garage's rear ramp. The aft fifteen feet of the transport—his garage—housed his chocked-and-strapped 'forty-two Harley-Victory Road Commander, blacked-out from its handlebars to its thrusters.

He made his way back to the garage in seconds, boarded the bike in place and fired her up. When he jerked the thruster control to full *Aft Horizontal*, their position was confirmed on the dash screen above the bars. But he kept the throttle at a low idle and waited. Wind whipping in through the open tail created a maelstrom in the garage. *I sure wish I'd thrown on a hat and tied up my damn hair!*

The garage's interior was as black as the bike's paint and the invisible tunnel walls meters away in all directions. Brilliant road beams of the pursuing transport rendered the dim blue glow of his bike's idling thrusters insignificant.

Zaya's WristPad enabled him to raise or lower the garage's ramp door and to tweak the transport's cruising speed, but not its altitude. He assumed all that little-used finery still worked. Astride his Road Commander, he waited until his pursuers closed the gap to four lengths. Watched them via the bike's rear cam monitor on the dash screen. They must be on *cruise* too—nothing else seemed possible. Not willing to entrust his next moves to voice commands, he touched the transport's *Slow Ten Knots* button on his Wrist-Pad. Within two seconds, the bus responded with unquestioning obedience.

Zaya cranked the right handlebar grip that shot one hundred percent power to his bike's twin thrusters over the top of the horizontal ramp, blistering its paint. The pursuing transport flew into the hottest portion of twenty-foot white-hot hydrogen flames and stayed there long enough to melt its windscreen. Anyone or anything in the cockpit? Charbroiled in seconds. *Oops. Overkill. No answers tonight. Dead goons tell no tales. I do feel bad. Oh well....*

The gap widened an instant later. A sea of sparks showered the tunnel's interior from the now-roasted pursuers as they faded into a distant tumbling twinkle. Zaya killed the bike. The fifty-knot draft around the ramp sucked out the fumes in seconds. He touched the *Secure Ramp* button on his WristPad while rushing forward through his living and office areas, up the steps, and back into the cockpit once more. Just in time.

Sensors thought the tunnel ended up ahead. Or was it just a curve? The bus couldn't tell the difference. So it was screaming a warning. *God, I hate tunnels.* Throttling down too fast, his nose dipped before re-leveling. Zaya shifted *Thruster Attitude* to *All Vertical* again with a downward swipe on the dash and waved at *hover* a second later. Power dropped to five percent in response to the *LLH—Low-Level Hover—*command. *Cruise* might have handled this swift command sequence if he trusted it more. He didn't.

A ground check seemed prudent before he'd allow his dear old house and home to settle into the unknown. Besides, he needed time to think, to research this tunnel system. Even if the burning wreck of his pursuers didn't now block the way back, without room to turn around, the only practical egress lay ahead. Yes, he needed to pull up the relevant charts. If they existed.

An old journalist's adage crept into his mind: *Trust is sometimes necessary, but direct confirmation is essential.* So he cautiously cracked an inspection port in the floor toward the rear of the cockpit at the centerline. At least the steamy smell that accosted him from below, as foul as it was, didn't seem toxic, and no flowing liquid. Yet.

Time seemed suspended. He rubbed the back of his

sweaty neck with both hands after closing and locking the port. Energized by a few deep breaths, he leaped down the three steps from the cockpit. Three paces later he stood staring at his desk reviewing the events so far.

ZAYA'S HANDS TREMBLED. NOT FROM FEAR, BUT AN adrenaline hangover hit him like a suffocating fog. An annoying disequilibrium forced him to gravity-drop into the chair on a floor-mounted pedestal at his starboard-side workstation. *Damn, I'm still alive!*

His obedient screens awaited. Because of his basic distrust of voice control, his fingers flew over a keyboard under each hand. *Well, that's interesting....* Analysis proved the ground solid with only a nine percent average instability beneath all projected jack sites. Acceptable. Instead of returning to the cockpit, he lowered just four support jacks from his WristPad. He'd not be staying here long, but saw no reason to plant his tires into this sewer muck and whatever else lived down here. Nor did he need all eight jacks. Plus these days he only operated essential equipment. Besides, it made no sense to expose his still red-hot thrusters to something too nasty to be healthy. They needed time and space to cool. And since the altimeter said he'd descended a hundred meters over the last kilometer, no telling when the stormy skies outside might open up and flash-flood these tunnels.

Zaya expelled a sigh of relief. *The old girl performed with aplomb, even though she ate some dirt. Now another fricking repair bill I can't afford...*

"*Who are you calling 'an old girl?'*"

A surprising laugh escaped. *Sorry, PodGirl. Not you... it's this needy old bus. Thanks for the heading. Now how do I get out of here?* No response. On his own. *Have I pissed you off with my driving? Or...? God, if you only knew how much... What am I saying? You know.* Zaya slumped in the reflected teal glow of the cockpit's instrumentation that lit his left shoulder. And the softer orange glow from the array of indicator lights in the panel overhead along with those in front of him. He needed illumination.

HE HAD WANTED TO QUESTION THOSE GOONS, BUT FAILED. Allowed his emotion to run away. They held a key to unlocking the mystery he had chased for over a year, but since they all died by thruster roast, he'd dig out another angle. He always did. His year-long investigation into several murders revealed a vague connection between them. Now, Zaya's podcasts had generated sufficient buzz to move his name in some villain's ledger from the annoyance column to the problem-elimination column. He had captured unwanted attention from Proconsul Libby Blade's goon squad. If he could just survive this day....

Zaya planned his egress from this tunnel. He pulled up chart after chart, but they revealed nothing helpful. So he stared at vague blueprints on the two-meter screen that arose from the back edge of his ebony desk, reflecting in the blue-green glow how all this started. His antennae had begun to tingle before he first became involved two years ago when he had leaped into this preposterous plot....

2

———

O LD WASHINGTON,
   MARYGINIA
   MAY 2148

LUCY SLOUCHED. ALONE. IN THE SMALL READING ROOM, SHE admitted to herself the Georgetown Library was her sanctuary. Again. How many thousands of hours had she spent here over the last few years? She loved the smell of old paper-bound books and the yellowish lighting reminiscent of long-obsolete and now-outlawed candescent lamps. This earthy place of long tables and endless walls of books, including actual books printed on real paper, felt like it should be dusty and musty, but it was spotless. Still....

The quiet and cozy room shut out at least some of the mental clutter causing her sleepless nights ever since she intercepted one voxmail that changed everything. Sometimes, she'd just drop her head to the table on a book or a keyboard and slept when her eyes disobeyed her will. Now, when not dozing, her every motion remained focused, hurried, and urgent. Even though every cell deep within her primal lizard brain compelled her to run and hide, she did not.

Lucy Candelson, aide-de-camp to Proconsul Elizabeth Blade of the United Westican Territories twenty-eighth Assembly of Elders, seemed unstoppable. At twenty-four, Lucy's star shone brightly. She had achieved her Masters degree in Political Science from Georgetown in less than a year. That was two years ago—an eternity. Now, with the priceless experience and prestige of working for the influential proconsul? Her matchless work ethic and ambitious demeanor, coupled with an eidetic memory and unforgettable pixie features, represented the complete package of an up-and-coming political fast-tracker.

Lucy loved the Alliance and worked to make it better. That's why she sought a career in politics. As a closet environmental activist, however, she led a double life. She wanted to change the system from within, but the system was swallowing her. It started with her incidental access to that after-hours voxmail to her boss from a cabinet member —the Secretary of Defense, Madeleine Haley. In her message, Secretary Haley apologized for egregiously breeching security protocol by leaving such a bombshell in a vox message. She said she had her reasons. Lucy told no one what she had heard, not even her boss, until she could learn more, but dared not delete the message either.

So on her own, Lucy dedicated herself to discovering the heights to which this obvious conspiracy ascended. What she learned left her stunned. Proconsul Blade's ambition scaled a ruthless dimension she could not comprehend, it seemed. Lucy thought, *I admire Libby as a strong female role model, but this!*

She spent most of her scarce free time on the familiar Georgetown University campus far from the Capitol's prying eyes across the river. Close to her home near the water, her infinitely patient stay-at-home husband awaited. But Lars' limits were not boundless. If only she could tell him of her suspicions, but that would only put him in danger too.

Lucy sifted through endless data related to telecommunications, climatology, and the science of electromagnetic waves. Lucy could only describe her discovery as a preposterous abuse of political power. The most appalling dimension? Somebody created the opportunity for an Alliance-sponsored public health hazard on a global scale—a technology-driven pandemic, or worse. Despite her own ambition, it appalled Lucy to learn of a horrifying conspiracy comprising a strategy developed by the Grandy Group, a non-Alliance organization, or NAO. They once called them NGOs. A disenfranchised policy guy within Grandy was the key. Then he turned up dead. *Suicide? No way.*

Lucy's doubt consumed her. Was her boss a party to some or all of this dreadful plot? She could not deny her strong suspicions, though she tried. *Proconsul Blade takes part in too many off-calendar meetings and secret voxcons. And that snake Mayfield Bailey from Gray and Foster Telecom Consulting? Whenever I enter the proconsul's office, why do the two of them fall silent and share furtive glances?*

Once, she met Anderson Dean from the Capitol Security Service whom she disliked for no good reason. Her instincts? He was little more than an ivy league thug in a five-thousand-dollar suit. Oh, he's slick, alright, but something about him caused the hairs on the back of her neck to bristle when he was in the room. *And why so many calls between Madame Proconsul and this guy, but never face-to-face? They both work in the Capitol.*

Lucy continued torturing herself with this endless line of self-interrogation. *So why does Proconsul Blade feel it necessary to surround herself with such unsavory characters if she is innocent? Just how far does political expediency carry one's ethics into darkness?*

Knowing she could trust no one, Lucy took unilateral action to research Secretary Haley's fears. She imagined the secretary was in for a rough ride too. Counter to the secretary's beliefs, Proconsul Blade's position on the AE8897 bill before the Assembly of Elders was no secret, but the scaffolding it apparently provided for high treason, was. Lucy harbored no doubt she needed to bring her frightening suppositions into the light of day. That remained her only option, no matter the risk. Someone was playing a very serious game with the highest stakes. The warm and welcoming ambience of the Georgetown Library Reading Room had grown bone-chilling.

Her decision made, Lucy realized she must confide in someone. But who to trust? Certainly nobody in politics. She scanned the twenty-four-hour-access room. Only a few others shared the smallish space with her this late. She committed to pass her private journal to her new friend, Lamatte Foliére. She knew she was in mortal danger and needed a backstop. *And he is still here.*

"Lamatte, may I have a word in private?"

3
____

N EW WASH, MARYGINIA

____

"You don't really want to shoot me, do you?" Moments earlier, Zaya French felt more than heard the throaty charging cycle of the small but lethal pulse pistol pressed hard against his lower back. His cold faux-leather waistcoat creaked in protest. The assailant's other hand gripped Zaya's left shoulder. The oblivious crowd on the platform rushed past in the dim light made hazy by airborne pollutants. A normal New Wash evening. Masks muffled their voices.

"French, you had no right to publicize my relationship with the Grandy Group, or that Assembly aide." He gasped as if his nervous energy was consuming him, "That was to remain private and personal. Now I am a dead man. And I may not be the only one." Lamatte Foliére's resolve quavered. He was no killer, but his anger consumed him after listening to Zaya's latest journal posting. He sensed something else plagued the would-be killer.

Stray hairs danced across Zaya's forehead, dancing to the pressure wave of the passing train. Scraps of plastipaper stirred up from the dirty platform to take flight.

"Damn it, French, my gut tells me you are an enemy willing to slaughter your own mother for a juicy lead. I trusted you. Give me one good reason..." The man teetered on the brink of tears. His voice shook as much as his hands as he pressed the weapon harder into the small of Zaya's back. His intuition screamed at him

Something else, but what?

"Okay, listen, Lamatte, let me make this right." With deliberate care, he eased away from the trembling hand on his shoulder. Pivoting to his right, Zaya looked into his eyes less than a foot distant. The desperation Zaya saw and heard shook his confidence. Lamatte Foliére was a man balanced on a crumbling edge. They might both go over. Together. "Look... Lamatte... I can't un-publish, but I can further camouflage your involvement next week. But only if I'm alive to do so, okay? Let me do this for you."

The tears flowed now. Foliére's commitment to violence eroded into uncertainty as he his dropped chin to his chest. The little knuckle gun at the end of his muscled arm grew heavy as it succumbed to gravity and despair. After several moments of quiet sobbing, he even allowed Zaya to offer him a supportive man-hug as the weapon disappeared into the folds of his robes. His tears ran like rivers down his neck and chin onto his soiled clerical collar.

4

———

CHICAGO,
WILLIANA
UNITED WESTICAN TERRITORIES
MAY 2149

———

DETECTIVE LIONEL SMITH OF THE CHICAGO ENFORCEMENT Department caught the day's AirQual rating of seven an hour earlier on one of the local feeds he monitors. That concerned him. He suffered from asthma and at least six chronic allergies. So did his three kids. And three decades of mutating virulent pandemics hadn't made life easy for anyone in the UWT. None more so than little Annie. Broke his heart how she struggled to breathe—mask or no mask. Even inside, house-wide filtered array or not. A trickle always helped, but who could afford a constant oxygen trickle in a mask, much less a whole-house flow on a cop's salary?

Masks were as ubiquitous as noses and mouths. And

"mask rash" was the new common cold. Smitty learned something from one of his science feeds last night. Just two centuries ago, Earth's atmosphere comprised over twenty percent oxygen. Now it was about thirteen percent and still dropping. With Annie, some other symptoms got worse in the last few months too. But nobody knew what caused them. No time to dwell on that right now. This was sure to be a huge case.

Smitty said, "Geez, this air slows me down. Gotta be the worst in all of Westica."

His beautiful boss purred, her voice made thick by her mask, "Not just you, Smitty. Slows everything down. Hey, have you lost some weight, big guy?" The chagrined Detective Smith visualized his dear wife of twenty years slaving over her ancient sewing machine to let out the waistline of today's trousers. *But I'm tall and carry my bulk well, don't I? And now Captain Drop-Dead-Gorgeous is complimenting me? Jeez.*

"I shed a few pounds, Cap. Not enough." A blushing school boy kicking sand in the playground. *Double-jeez.*

EARLIER THAT MORNING BEFORE ANOTHER HAZY SUNRISE, A voxcon had pulled CED Captain Judge Miners out of a warm bed. An hour later she was still waking up at the scene clutching a huge travel mug of rocket fuel.

As she slid out of her flat-black transport five blocks south of Lakeshore Drive on a jagged side street, her no-nonsense hair with white-blonde bangs still clung to her forehead in disobedient clumps from a quick shower and a quicker comb. The captain's edgy green eyes hovered above high cheek bones and pouty lips. At five-nine, her creamy figure commanded stares from both men and women alike. Blessed with beauty, she never flaunted it.

Every time she met someone for the first time and got that quizzical look regarding her unique moniker, she issued her practiced response. "My parents prided themselves on their practical sense of humor. I'm third-generation policy enforcement, and they thought an unusual name—like Judge—would serve me well in the family business. I suppose they were right." She always followed that response with a self-deprecating smirk. That was the captain.

As on-scene commander, Captain Miners asked, "Wadda we got?" after ordering everyone to "Cinch your damn masks, people! And up your trickle. You know the drill. We don't need any passed-out cops in front of all these suits." The captain achieved a challenging Master's Degree in Criminology with a double minor in Forensic Psychology and Linguistics from Northwestern. Still, she used street vernacular with her street team. They rewarded her with fanatic loyalty.

"A dumpster-diving homeless person stumbled upon the sotted victim down that dead-end alley, Captain." The young officer's body language signaled he might lose his breakfast into his mask, and turned away to collect himself.

She'd been briefed that several local, state, and Alliance policy enforcement agencies, were now on site and on high alert including CED, Alliance Marshals, the Secret Service, and the Alliance Intelligence Agency—which was similar to the FBI in old America. A few other agencies of lesser repute arrived and hovered at the periphery. Someone even whispered the word, *terrorism,* but someone else rumored to be an AIA agent told them to *shut the Hell up.* Once they identified the victim, they re-classified an otherwise-anonymous ghetto murder as an assassination and a matter of Alliance security.

A shotgun blast to her face prevented immediate identification. Naked, gutted and nothing but stumps and pieces remained—no hands or feet. Didn't matter. The murderer wasn't trying to prevent an identification, but sent a message. Those facts alone made it a newsworthy story.

CAPTAIN MINERS OFFERED HER THANKS TO THE WELL-equipped CED Scene Investigation Team for their quick ID of the high-profile victim who they determined was Madeleine Haley, the sitting Secretary of Defense of the United Westican Territories. The captain directed two dozen beat cops to canvass the surrounding neighborhoods while other agencies carved out well-segregated tasks.

Since this was a local homicide, CED took the lead—with more Alliance help than made sense. The rationale: leverage local knowledge and contain the political fallout.

Not much escaped the public eye. Dozens of levitation craft—levs—from various news agencies hovered overhead in funereal silence. The feeds went viral. Chaos reigned, at least for one news cycle—all ten minutes of it.

The captain stood outside the on-site command vehicle despite the bitter lake breeze that attacked her clean-shaven neck. No hat or neck wrap. Big mistake. Smitty and a young uniformed officer headed her way.

"Captain Miners? You'll want to hear this. Officer M'Dala, tell the Captain what you found."

At first, the officer's voice sounded strong and confident. "Sir, during our canvass, we discovered the entrance to a bird cage. We interviewed three birds in a basement."

"Captain, birds are folks who believe we are being inundated by poisonous electromagnetic waves. They protect themselves with metal shielding like copper screen. That's why they call them birds in cages."

"Smitty, I know who birds are, and that they sometimes call us frogs—ignorant, in a pot, and on a slow boil, but thanks."

"Sorry, Cap. Officer, please continue."

"Well, sir, we pieced this together. No eye witnesses, but we have two ear witnesses. From a basement near the scene. A broken window led to the street. One bird described hearing the words, 'She oughta be pleased,' and 'Rudest job for SS yet.'"

"Thanks, Officer. When you attempted to detain those witnesses for further questioning... tell the captain."

Through her CED-issued mask, the almost-inaudible hiss of the O2 valve punctuated Officer M'Dala's halting speech. She did not want to disappoint this great lady. "Well, sir, uh, those two young birds accompanied by an older lady reluctantly offered their testimony and then, uh, scurried off in the dark." Her next words tumbled out faster and higher-pitched. "We were not expecting that. We gave chase, but we, uh, we lost them." The officer fell quiet, cast her eyes downward.

"Alright, Officer M'Dala. Can't say I'm not disappointed. These are good leads. Smitty?"

"Yes, ma'am. We're scouring that basement, but—"

"I understand. Ask the team to stay on it. Not much hope though, right?"

"No, ma'am."

THAT WAS A YEAR AGO. ZAYA HAD VOXCONNED HIS OLD FRIEND, Detective Lionel Smith. Smitty said, "That's how it played out that day. I'll never forget." The man sounded flat, like the fizz on that drink was long gone.

"You never solved Secretary Haley's murder." Not a question.

"Nah. It never went anywhere after that, old buddy. They're still riding the Captain. Hard. But nobody else has solved it either. Anyway, this one was way above my pay grade from the get-go. All the agencies' blustering, still, and even the captain's best efforts came up with zilch."

So Zaya described his own white whale—actually, several. "I'm wondering if this old case of yours might relate to my own investigation. Betting it does."

Smitty always had the nose of a bloodhound, and would never suggest giving up on a cold case. Despite the different *signature* of the secretary's murder, if this was the same killer using a different MO, the secretary's death could be the latest and most visible in a series of mysterious deaths. Zaya took the aging detective into his confidence. Smitty agreed, with certain reservations, to that possibility.

Zaya appreciated talking this out with his old friend. "The killer or killers meant the other deaths to look like unrelated accidents and suicides of scientists, minor politicos, and business leaders. Then, this prominent Alliance official? Near a once-exclusive address fallen from grace? Does this not scream of symbolism, Smitty? But what the Hell does it symbolize?"

"Look, man, I don't know from symbolism. Can only follow the evidence, especially on a string of cold ones like these,"

"Yeah, you're right, of course."

If he was going to crack this nut, Zaya knew he needed

to think more like a cop. Evidence. The Haley case. Might be the key. He lived in Chicago for two years. He knew the heart of Lakeshore Drive, once a swanky neighborhood of high-rises, bordered one of North America's five great lakes —Lake Michigan. Once great, it used to be beautiful, now a cesspool of humanity's leftovers. The stench alone drove affluent urbanites and commensurate commerce farther west. The part of Lakeshore near the murder site was now a wasteland, a refuge for the lower castes. A honeycomb of old sub-basements, walking tunnels, and abandoned train tunnels still meandered underneath new basements of newer buildings. They called that now-dead region on the hill a half-mile south of the lake, 'Old Chicago.'

Zaya's feed-scanning bots might not have brought this grisly murder to his attention other than to satisfy his sense of morbid curiosity. Those soul-less chunks of software knew him too well. He had already connected several deaths and the circumstances surrounding them, as obscure as those connections were. That took some serious digging. Was the Alliance defense secretary's death related too? He thought so, and Smitty agreed, although his cop's nose still itched. Zaya was on the hunt and added this case to his portfolio of suspicious events.

For the last year, the gruesome nature of the secretary's disfigurement had begged so many questions. Was this a message of unknown meaning? To whom? And for what purpose? As a cabinet-level Alliance official, the investigators—at least the feds—had to assume someone tortured her for classified secrets. If so, which ones? And why? Did this murder even relate to Zaya's investigation? Did this represent an escalation? Or was it nothing more than a vendetta driven by an unknown motive?

Zaya needed to get his head around the logic of this

"case" now almost a year downrange of the secretary's bizarre murder. His instincts screamed at him. His hypothesis had merit: five mysterious deaths seemed connected to a single conspiracy of some sort.

He summarized his thinking, as he had shared it with Smitty....

Five months before the defense secretary's death, in January, an obscure climatologist who was a professor at Cornell, committed suicide in his Ithaca, New York home. His daughter, Cecile, a dear friend, confided in Zaya. More than that, Cecile appealed to him for help. "No way Daddy killed himself," she told him with such conviction that he believed her. Besides, Zaya knew her to be the very bedrock of rational thought. *One additional aside. I could refuse Cecile nothing. Ever.*

A month later, in February, a renewable energy executive in the Washegon territory fell victim to a near-fatal accident outside of Portland. The family later pulled the plug. Cecile called when she heard that news. She informed Zaya her father knew this energy guy. From that and voxcon records, Zaya discovered Cecile's father and the energy guy shared several confidential conversations just before their respective tragedies. No way *that* was a coincidence. By that point, with his scanners sounding alarms, Zaya had become obsessed with what he called his "stump case." He remain stumped with more questions than answers, but stayed on the trail.

Another month passed before intuition—fed by Zaya's scan-bots—told him a Calexico telecom executive who turned up dead in his bathtub did not die accidentally either. While they ruled that death in Palo Alto a suicide, myriad questions remained. That was in March.

Smitty had asked, "And how many dead-end alleys have

you abandoned because your overactive imagination slammed your nose into brick walls?"

"Let's not even go there. I know this is convoluted, but indulge me. I mapped all this out on the wall screen in my transport—my motorhome—to keep it straight in my mind. And here's one last piece to this puzzle. I found a connection among these three victims last December. Remember that telecom exec of the Silicon Valley conglomerate, the Grandy Group? The Palo Alto *bathtub suicide?* He had signed up to speak at the same media conference attended by the scientist and the energy exec in Fort Dallas. Curiouser and curiouser, right?"

"Well, I got nothin' for ya, Z." Smitty sounded disappointed he couldn't be more helpful. Zaya could tell his friend thought he was nuts. Like everyone else.

So ZAYA FRENCH, ERSTWHILE SELF-PROFESSED INVESTIGATIVE journalist did what all journalists do when jammed up. He published what he knew to his expansive online subscribers and all the true crime feeds, hoping to shake something loose. His recent *Redemption Alley* journal sounded like this:

"You know me by now, right? If you've been hanging around here long enough, you cannot imagine I'm one of those conspiracy nuts. That does not mean conspiracies do not exist. Considering this case's *stumpiness,* I want this one solved. I'm tired of being stumped for so long.

"Two months after the Grandy manager's alleged suicide, the husband of a young assembly aide discovered his wife's body in their Georgetown condo. Overdose. He told me she never used drugs. Quite the opposite. She revered her body, her relationship with her husband whom she adored, and her political career. I discovered yet another anomaly concerning Lucy Candelson—one of Proconsul Elizabeth Blade's aides. My source informs me Candelson's online searches sought a direct correlation between telecom lobbyists and toxic electromagnetic pollution on a global scale. Now why would an assembly aide from the great territory of Montanaho research such a correlation? For weeks, this conscientious aide was a frequent flyer at the Georgetown University library and archives in Old Washington—so reported to me by one of their volunteer curators. And why use one of the library's public-access puters instead of one of her own private or Alliance-issued devices?

"Look, sometimes my methods are dubious, treating certain laws as guidelines. I have many friends. I learned the aide attempted three calls to our dead Grandy executive. What in this particular circle of Hell was going on? But Secretary Haley's murder diverged from the modus operandi of these earlier casualties. Despite the different MO, would I find a connection? Now, a year downrange of SecDef's murder in Chicago, my humble investigative efforts lit up someone's alerts. I had made no secret of investigating these five deaths. Why should I? Writers perform research. Examine *any* author's search history and you might think he or she capable of murder, sedition, terrorism, acts of random kindness, bestiality, or worse. It's just research, folks."

Zaya thought, *Well, now I rather wish subtlety was one of my character defects because I've become some unknown party's target. But I am done kicking my derrière for this obvious indiscretion. My current mandate? Personal survival.*

NOT HAVING LEARNED HIS LESSON, OR BEING SO OBSESSED with shaking loose clues, Zaya broadcast another episode of his *Redemption Alley* journal.

"If you were around a month ago, you learned I was the victim of an attempted mugging—an armed robbery—in rural Pennsylvania, if you can believe that. I did not go gently into that good night. I kicked that mugger's ass before he escaped. After acquiring a few bruises, but with my ego and physiology intact, and after some post-action analysis, I realized this was no random mugging. More like attempted murder made to *appear* something like a mugging gone wrong.

"Two weeks ago near New Wash, I met with a curator— one of several—of the Georgetown University archives and reading room. I alluded to that encounter in my last episode of *The Alley*. Father Lamatte Foliére had personally observed the proconsul's aide visiting his reading room during countless visits over the course of the first few weeks in May. He even formed a casual relationship with her. I quizzed the priest on the deceased aide's efforts in his library. She had asked him for research ideas and materials on the Grandy Group and on several New Wash lobbyists. She zeroed in on one guy named Mayfield Bailey, whose exclusive client is— wait for it—Grandy.

"She also focused her research on Grandy's policy history. One executive within that discipline stood out. Guess who? Yup, the Grandy executive, Seamus Harstowe, reported dead in March of last year in his home in Palo Alto, Calexico. Another alleged suicide. So, my friends, do you see where this is going? The curator couldn't or wouldn't tell me much more. But too many arrows pointed at Grandy. And last week, I thought this Jesuit priest, the Georgetown reading room curator, meant to kill me. He confronted me on the Bush Street lev train platform in New Wash after digesting that week's broadcast of *The Alley*. It shocked me how desperate he was to keep his trivial involvement in this entire affair a secret.

"So five deaths spanning six months of last year are likely connected. Someone has gone to extraordinary measures to make sure these deaths appear unrelated, accidental, or suicidal, except for the secretary's violent demise. The five victims' interests or expertise span climatology, energy, communications, academia, and the Alliance. And now I am a target.

"The good news? I *must* be on the right track. The bad news? The trail is growing chilly even as it grows more dangerous. Then, last night, Father Foliére left me a voxcon just before he disappeared.

What's next? *Who's* next?"

5

N EW WASH,
MARYGINIA
2150

Andrea Davies, a rabid fan of true crime shows, listened to the latest episode of the *Redemption Alley* journal. Shocked, Libby Blade's Chief of Staff brought it to her boss's attention.

"You're joking! Thank you, Andy. Please get a secure voxcon to Anderson Dean."

"Yes, ma'am."

While she waited, like the gruesome scene of an accident demands you stare as you hover past, her disbelief and horror compelled her to listen to this entire podcast, or audio journal, or whatever the hell it was. Then she listened to it again while waiting for Andy to locate and connect that weasel from Security.

"Agent Dean, are you paying attention to the broadcast of this *Redemption Alley* journal on the feeds?"

"Madame Proconsul?"

She kicked closed her office door with a sideways glance as she checked her own reflection in the glossy wall to her right—her good side. "Oh, for chrissake, Anderson, get your head out of your ass. This Zaya French is laying out most of our strategy for our 8897 legislation. And he's incriminating us! Andy tells me he has a loyal following. This guy claims it's entertaining fiction, but he uses actual names and he's reporting facts, including your 'secret' job with your mob of thugs! Anderson, defuse the situation, now, but no 'tip of the spear' crap on this one. This guy's already gone public. The last thing we need is to add fuel to these conspiracy flames."

"Yes, ma'am."

Madame Proconsul of the Assembly of Elders hung up and listened to the entire podcast, or journal, or whatever, one more time.

6

Undisclosed Location

Zaya had already begun broadcasting with his customary monologue. Anyone could listen live or download his audio journal from any of the worldwide feeds. Listeners couldn't get enough of his unique blend of true crime facts with entertaining—fictional—overtones. His voice broke with excitement and short sentences that he rushed to get out before it was too late.

"Look, folks, I continue to dig. But I have yet to identify who is trying to wave me off. Five people are dead, and their deaths are related. But nobody else seems to have made the same connection. Why? A specific motive eludes me. But I *am* getting closer. Were these five unfortunates party to some conspiracy or exposé? Did they suffer from an attack of conscience that made them loose ends? Or did they get greedy? And who gains from silencing them?"

Zaya sidled up closer to the microphone protruding from the broadcast console in his transport. He verified he was still recording and transmitting. Checked his levels and signal strength. All still in the green. Good.

"Let's review: First, the legislation soon up for a vote known as AE8897 includes provisions for re-tasking satellites away from *climate* change research. Read for yourself the cryptic and voluminous public domain draft of that bill. Corpse number one in early 2149 was a *climatologist*.

"Second, an *energy* executive fell victim to a single-vehicle transport accident. He and the climatologist were acquaintances. He was corpse number two and buried a month after the climate expert died.

"Third, 8897 involves re-tasking satellites to enable emerging *communication* technology. Corpse number three in that same year was a business policy executive at a tele*communication* firm.

"Fourth, an *Assembly* aide overdoses after she connected lobbying efforts and significant money transfers to buttress this same piece of new legislation. She was corpse number four on that same timeline last year.

"Fifth, an influential and vocal *opponent of 8897*? UWT Secretary of Defense Madeleine Haley. Corpse number five.

"Sixth, one influential legislator—the prime mover of 8897—is being aggressively lobbied by the tele*communications* lobby. Coincidence?

"And finally, except for the secretary, *the deceased all knew each other.* I have personal testimony, phone records, and evidence of their meetings during 2148 and 2149 to corroborate this assertion."

As the broadcast continued, Zaya's objective changed from reviewing irrefutable evidence to inciting a reaction from Libby Blade herself. He knew she or someone on her staff would be listening. "Madame Proconsul, I invite you to help me see the error of my ways. My mind remains open, even armed with these seven data points. Your unwillingness to provide your perspective to date is revealing. Perhaps you are too busy to set this humble storyteller straight. Or you've dismissed me as another conspiracy wing-nut. But is not my evidence too compelling? Or perhaps you're just not a fan."

He heard a noise outside. Not a good sign. Time to wind up this episode before it was too late.

"Dear listeners, I am not yet prepared to declare anything more than suppositions at this point. But the sketch is evolving into a drawing. I am getting close. I even received an anonymous warning to stop. This is revealing because I have referred to this investigation only in this journal to you, dear listeners. That means one of *you* is nervous. Time for me to move again. Too hot here anyway. Until next time, this is Zaya French signing off."

7

———

NEW WASH, MARYGINIA 2150

THE STEAMY NEW WASH SUMMER PRESSED IN ON ANYONE caught in the open. Dressed in loose-fitting shorts with a hooded sweatshirt and a mask covering most of his face underneath a floppy hoody, Zaya walked north on the wide Fourth Street sidewalk at a brisk pace. The mid-ankle specialty trainers dangled from around Zaya's neck suggested he was looking for more than weight training. Turning to his left, he entered a small building tucked between two ancient ultra-rises. Glancing over his right shoulder as he entered, he took casual note of a row of vacant industrial buildings across the semi-busy boulevard. A crappy neighborhood on the verge of re-gentrification. Again.

. . .

ZAYA HAD BEEN A GYM RAT HIS ENTIRE LIFE. AT FIVE-FOOT-five, he was shorter than most. And self-confident to a fault. Kids still picked on him when he was younger. As he bulked out, that happened less. Besides, his ability to bullshit his way out of fights improved. That and his ineffable charm.

If you asked him, Zaya would say, "Look, the real reason I treat my body like a temple? Major serial cardiac events took both my father and paternal grandfather before the age of eighty. I will be seventy in four short months. Food for serious thought." He tossed his damp sweatshirt by the free-weight rack beside his bottle of electrolytes. His sleeveless T covered as much as it could. The poor thing stretched to its limits by Zaya's well-muscled body. It was an old T-shirt.

THE GUY LOOKED AT ZAYA'S NAKED BICEPS AND SAID, "GEEZ, man, you got some major league guns.'" He had just met Davey minutes earlier. Here at the Fourth Street Boxing Club in Southeast New Wash, Davey was working his own biceps with a set of bells on the bench next to Zaya on the club's padded free-weight floor. Grimy windows out onto Fourth flooded the front of the gym with hazy natural light. The air in here was decent. Perpendicular to the windows on their left, floor-to-ceiling mirrors stared back at them so they could analyze their workout form.

Zaya was damn proud of a rock-hard thirty-four-inch waste that accentuated his broad shoulders, chiseled abs, arms, and back. Color him proud for working hard over the years to achieve this. A few scars on his upper arms begged questions few asked about. He could explain away some of the wrinkles, but couldn't ignore his... laugh lines. *Yeah, that's what they are,* he told himself, *laughable.*

"Thanks, Davey. All natural, brother. No juice cuz I wanna have kids some day." A joke. Davey just nodded like he understood. He didn't. Or if he did, he didn't care. Zaya always wanted kids, but that ship had long sailed.

"I hear ya, bro. You still fight?" Davey leaned into the question posed to his new lifting buddy, a near-leer on his face. The voice sounded like he kept at least one cheek stuffed full of marbles. All Brooklyn, that voice.

"Well, I know a few moves. I can take care of myself. But nah, not in the ring. Wanna keep my pretty face intact. I respect good technique but I'm more of an appreciative spectator."

Watching fighters go at it? Not my idea of a good time either. But no sense alienating my new buddy, and a potential source. "Hey, Davey. I hear some guys who work inside the new Beltway hang around the best gyms. Anybody like that here?"

"Oh, sure. Lots of 'em. They come down here to butch up. Hang with tough guys. Get sweaty. Makes 'em feel like they're not pussies. Some 'er gay or trans and need to defend themselves more'n most. Joey K over there, he teaches 'em a few moves."

"K?"

"Yeah. The K is short for *Knockout*. Joey's famous around here for his blackout choker move. You get too close, you're done. He used to be a decent cage fighter, but he got hurt real bad. Now he's a *personal trainer*. Them yuppies get off on that. Tough guy wannabes hangin' out with a bull stud. I don't have a lot in common with that type, and most can't box for shit, so no sense sparrin' with 'em. Or they got their snob noses crammed up each others' asses. Know what I mean?"

"Yeah. Sorry I'm not your guy for sparring either."

"Hey, that's cool. At least you're the real deal. How much you press, anyway, dude?"

From one careful glance at the guy, it was obvious Joey 'K' Gainer took on all comers in his day. He seemed to wear his cauliflower ears and portobello nose like badges of honor. A short tank of a guy with a shiny head, Joey carried a big chip on his shoulder. At least that's what Zaya saw from across the room as he worked Davey for more background info. Hard to hide under bright vapor lights. Joey K stood out. Davey told Zaya that Joey never backed down. Never needed to. As hazardous as jagged steel. He warned Zaya not to stand too close or to make any sudden moves. *Geez.* Davey swaggered across the gym floor with Zaya in tow at a respectable distance.

"Yo, Joey! I want you to meet a new friend of mine, Zaya French. Zaya's one of us, man, not one of them pussy lobbyists you babysit."

In a fierce half-whisper, Joey said, "Keep your voice down, kid! Business is business. Unlike you, Davey, those pussies pay their dues and they tip large." Another Brooklynite? Maybe Bronx. Joey lazily swiveled his knockout gaze toward Zaya who stood his ground a few feet away. Fifteen tense seconds passed. Nobody moved or spoke. They looked each other over—center-ring stares.

"A friend of Davey's.... Nice guns. You fight?"

"Zaya's a spectator, but he's seen some street action, right, Zaya?"

"Davey, why don't you shut up and let the man speak for himself?" A good-natured smirk, then smile, followed the jibe. Alpha to Beta, mentor to mentee, maybe.

Zaya didn't bother to shove a hand out. No need. Neither

did Joey. Such finery was for stiffs and suits. Zaya offered this brute his no-quarters body language, but in a congenial tone, said, "Hey, Joey. Davey's showing me the ropes."

"Yeah? By the look 'a ya, boy-o, you don't need no personal trainer though, am I right?"

"Well, I can always use a few more tips Just trying to be neighborly."

"You spar, Zaya?"

"Nah. I like to watch." He grinned at the double entendre wasted on these boys. And that was okay.

"Davey here says you're a player. So what's the deal? This here's a boxing club. C'mon, let's play. Don't worry. Nobody's gonna take out them nice pearly whites. My boy Davey here needs a workout. Ya game, boy-o?"

This was *not* how I saw my morning unfolding, but I needed info. What the Hell. "Davey, you get your workout on my gut, not my face so much. Fair enough?" Zaya counted on his forty-minute relationship to save his butt. *And* on saving his dental implants worth twenty grand.

The grizzly young fighter grinned, a shark inhaling chum. "Absolutely!" His mop of red hair—cut high 'n tight around the ears—bobbled as he nodded with greedy vigor. Or was he shaking from internal laughter at the prospect of comical carnage?

ZAYA GEARED UP WITH JOEY'S HELP. NO TAPE, JUST GLOVES, token headgear, and an ill-fitting pink mouthpiece that smelled of old cigarettes and something else. His awkward entrance into the ring became gym-wide amusement. No doubt the hawks drooled over the spectacle of the slaughter to come. This might be a regular form of entertainment here. Within minutes, Joey had Davey taped, tight, and tied, ready to rock the house—and Zaya. *What bloody mess have I gotten myself into now?* Zaya figured if he landed no vicious blows that Davey would reciprocate in kind. He was wrong.

"Okay, boys, nothin' fancy. Just a good-effort workout here. Davey, you don't want to kill your new friend. You're pacing here. Foot and body work. Step in, jab, fade back, work around. None 'a your wildman antics here, okay? Davey, you listenin' to me? *Davey!*"

Zaya's sparring partner danced in the ring and snorted through his nose like a rutting bull with a stick up his ass and loving it. Davey mumbled through a thick lisp around the edges of the mouthpiece half hanging out of his mouth. It caused a thick lisp. He grumbled, never taking his eyes off of mine, "Yeah, a'right already, Joey. Got it! Just a good-effort workout. And Zaya, I won't hurt ya too bad, man. You're a sport!" That leer again.

Joey stood on the gym floor below them near the ring's corner with the distant window wall behind him. Planted his right foot on a beat-up old stool. Hunching forward expectantly, he said, "Let's go."

Zaya realized he didn't know Davey at all, right after they faced off center canvas and engaged. In fact, he suspected these two suckered him into sparring from the moment he'd walked in from Fourth Street to sign up for a month-to-month membership. A hazing thing? *Shit.*

Fifteen lightning minutes later, with his pearly whites still intact, Zaya crawled from the ring below the bottom rope and stumbled down onto the gym floor. He rolled onto his back and stretched out flat. Most unmanly of him, he guessed. Not much blood on his t-shirt. Davey had been gentle. Reddened forearms from blocking Davey's blows, he had used defensive moves more than anything.

Still flat on his back and catching his breath, he dragged

his arms and legs apart in slow motion, then together again. As if he were making an imaginary snow angel. He guessed this would be a lighthearted sign of submission. Zaya French was not vying for the Alpha title today. More than a dozen others stood in a circle, towering over him, chuckling. So, near-comical sparring between a practiced pugilist and an aging street dog is cheap entertainment here? Got it. Most of the sweaty spectators now grinned slantways at each other and down at Zaya as if he were road kill.

Still dancing in the ring as if his workout was just beginning, Davey craned his gaze under his bobbling red hair down at Zaya and at the ring of spectators. He cut loose with a guttural belly laugh around the mouthpiece now hanging from the corner of his grin. Others joined in. Echoes rang through the gym, an amphitheater designed by punch-drunk boxers. His speech still thick around his mouthpiece, Davey said, "Zaya, you slay me, little big man! You're okay! And you got a mean left. But your combos suck!"

Joey K stood over Zaya too. Offered a hand. He vice-gripped his right forearm above Zaya's still-gloved hand. "Yeah, you got moves, sport. More martial arts than boxing. I could see you wanted to use your feet. Good you didn't. Woulda confused Davey. And pissed him off." Under his breath as the others wandered off, with the possibility of bloodletting evaporated, Joey said, "Now tell me why you're really here, sport."

Zaya collected himself, spit out that hideous pink mouthpiece into Joey's open hand, and shed those sweaty gloves with some help. *This guy is sharper than he looks.* He met the expectant stare of Joey's rheumy eyes now inches away. "Joey, I live in a transport. I *am* looking for a gym to call home for the next couple of months. After that, I'll be rolling on down the road. It's what I do. But for now, I'm also keeping my ear to the ground for a few sleazy beltway types that I suspect are into some nasty stuff. And by nasty, I mean bordering on treason, or worse. You a patriot, Joey?"

His nostrils flared. "Hey, don't come in here and piss on my leg, dawg. 'A course I'm a patriot. Once a Marine, always a Marine. Ain't *nothin'* worse 'n treason in my book. Not even murder."

"Alright, brother. Semper Fi. So you okay with me hanging around for a while, working out in your club, just talking to a few folks while I pump iron? Even spar a little, maybe? Nothing disruptive."

Make or break time. The lead dog spoke. "Well... sure, why not? But don't drive my customers away. Or you'll be dippin' your stick in my living, and we'll have trouble. And don't even *think* about callin' what you just did with Davey boxing."

"Deal. Thanks, Joey."

"Why you doin' this, man? For real?"

Zaya hoped he wasn't misreading this old junkyard dog. "I'm a writer, Joey. Freelance. I see bad stuff, I write about it. Maybe get it changed. That's it."

"Well, you're a good sport. And you can take care 'a yourself. Sorta. Not bad for an older guy."

"Older guy? Kiss my ass, Joey K. Besides, us old short guys gotta hang together, right?" Smiles all around. Davey was watching with an edge. Then he smiled too even though he hadn't heard a word.

"C'mere, boy-o." Joey pulled Zaya farther aside. Behind a heavy bag hanging from an exposed beam overhead. In a wheezing whisper, he said, "Zaya, I like you. A free word. Watch your back in here. Especially with that pretty boy."

He nodded toward a slick wearing a couple thousand bucks worth of gym clothes. "Name's Bailey. A nasty one, that. Loves sucker punches. Call's 'em a tactical advantage. Also the first to holler foul. You know the type."

"Deed I do, brother."

"And he hangs with a hitter name of Anderson Dean. An SS agent. Both lift and hit the bag. A lot. Never spar, though. Like they're buddies, but don't want folks to know that. Not here at the same time much, but when they are, 's like they're workin' too hard not to be seen together. I see, though."

"SS?"

"Also call 'em CSS—Capitol Security Service. A private outfit that gets paid to protect them politicians. Ask me, sport, they do a lot more 'n that."

"Meaning?"

"All I'm sayin.' Fer now, anyway. Enjoy your workout, boy-o."

"I owe you, Joey K."

"Yeah. You do. Be real careful with your curiosity 'round here, kid. I'm serious."

Zaya smiled. Damn near seventy years old and someone just called him *kid*.

8

———

N EW WASH, MARYGINIA

———

Father Lamatte Foliére cowered under a cloak of fear. He returned to his rectory where Georgetown University adjoined the sanctuary of St. Vroman's Sacred Heart Church near the tunnel under Freedom Boulevard. St. Vroman's was a small parish below street level where he was one of two priests in residence. The place was dark, cold. As he entered the ancient three-story structure of red brick, he looked up at the gambrel-style roof of copper grown green with verdigris a century earlier. Most windows were dark. This was home for now, but not for long.

As a priest-in-residence—not even a parochial vicar— Father Lamatte held no formal responsibilities other than honoring his spiritual retreat, and to officiate a few masses. But he held no administrative duties for the parish. He could not. The church's solution to his problem? Isolate and ignore. He agreed isolation was a sound strategy. But even left to negligence by the church, *he* could not ignore his condition. It frightened him. All the time. He could trust no one, so how could anyone trust him? And now, with the death of that nice young lady at the library....

Father Lamatte occupied a minuscule basement apartment in the small rectory. One other parish priest, Father Benedict Scolario, stayed in another dank apartment down the narrow central hall with two unoccupied apartments between them. St. Vroman's was a small impoverished parish. They could ill-afford a separate structure for their nunnery. Five nuns could occupy the second floor, but only two were in residence—the youthful Sister Maria and the elderly Sister Agatha whom anyone seldom saw. St. Vroman's flock had dwindled to a devout few.

Father Lamatte's mind was a prison, but his heart remained an open book. He and Sister Maria met in the musty first-floor library off the main entrance hall. Visiting priests sometimes meditated there. Dim lighting and long shadows fit hiss mood. They stood facing each other in a dark corner. Wanting to touch, but maintaining a respectful distance, Father Lamatte whispered the most difficult words he'd ever uttered. "Maria, we can do this no longer. Our vows...."

"Lamatte, what are you saying? This is difficult, but—" She looked up into his dewy eyes and saw what? Fear? She sensed a desperate edge to his voice. And something else.

"Maria, we can no longer see each other. I'm leaving."

Now *she* grew desperate. "No! Lamatte, we can serve our Lord *and* love each other, just like our flock. Why should we—"

"We cannot plod through that anemic discussion yet again. Our vows. We violated them and cheated on our marriage to the church. Besides, someone knows."

This caught her off-guard. Stunned. The hands folded in front of her that wanted to hold his took on a visible tremor. "What? What did you say, Lamatte?"

"A month ago I received a voxcon. It disguised the voice, but not his or her intentions. It directed me to do something, well, awful. Or they would expose our relationship. Since then, something even more awful found me, Maria. Now that will surface too. I must leave. You will never hear from me again. Goodbye, my love." With the back of his right hand he brushed her cheek just where it met the hood of her habit. He backed away, pulled from her reaching grasp. And swept from the room. A side portal led him to an alley exit without another word, his cassock trailing behind him like the shadowy specter he tried to escape.

Maria wept.

FATHER BENEDICT SCOLARIO SCOWLED. *GOOD RIDDANCE*, HE thought, as he observed the entire sordid scene from around a corner in the rectory's dusky hallway. They had whispered, but the old entry hall's superior acoustics just outside the library defeated their secrecy. *Father* Lamatte? What a joke. And with his dubious history? They should never have allowed him into the order. He knew things he shouldn't. How was that possible unless he was in league with dark powers? Ever since he heard Foliére's vile confession, he called for action. He served only the greater good and Mother Church. He muttered, "Godless criminals!" His brow furrowed so deep the wrinkles looked like a field plowed by a drunk. He pursed his thin lips so hard they turned a lighter shade of gray.

The ancient priest wheeled on his heels. His imperious brown cassock and long beige cincture billowed behind him. Their starched-stiff rustling brushed the intricate bas-relief paneling behind which he had cowered.

Bitterness comes with doing the wrong thing for the right reason.

Father Benedict knew he was the pious one, even though he had justifiably violated the vows of his confessional. His bitterness was bittersweet. But now, as he smiled with those rope-like lips in low contrast to his pasty face under the dim lights, he rushed back to the privacy of his room to place another important voxcon. These walls had ears.

———

LAMATTE FOLIÉRE'S FATHER, ANTOINE FOLIÉRE, HAD immigrated from French Algeria to Quebec City two decades earlier in a cloud of mystery with his motherless son. He found work as a laborer in Montreal when Lamatte was six. Lamatte's father taught him "Lamatte" is the French Quebecois derivation of the word, "Lamat." That name dripped with connotations of commitment and responsibility. Traced back to Borneo in the fifth or sixth century, the label of "Lamat" meant you were a librarian, a priest, or a keeper of tribal relics. You were a seeker of truth and wisdom. You saw your future lives. Others perceived you as an idealist illuminating a path to the future with the gifts of understanding and compassion.

Lamatte inherited much from his workaholic father, even his philosophy. He grew up in a religious household, just the two of them and the Roman Catholic church. That he would become a man of God seemed preordained. He wasn't sure, during rare moments if he was being honest with himself, whether this was his decision or his father's. More likely, both. The priesthood would be an escape. His lifestyle at home was restrictive because his father feared... what? But it seemed the Church was his destiny. He sought a desperate peace.

He remembered something old Father Benedict often said to anyone who would listen. *Bitterness comes with doing the wrong thing for the right reason.* That old priest wasn't happy *unless* he was bitter. So why was that stupid phrase now his personal ear worm? He knew why. Whatever else happened, Father Lamatte needed to protect Maria. He had never known such love. Not even with the Church. Now he'd need to distance himself from her, even though that felt wrong for the right reason. He wondered if old Benedict knew something he didn't.

As he trudged away from St. Vroman's down that rainy cobblestone street—more like an alley—an incoming voxcon startled him. His mask thickened his voice. "Hello?"

"We appreciate your continued cooperation to protect your lovely little Maria, Lamatte. Now *your* ass is on the line too."

That derisive tone pushed Lamatte's buttons to perfection. He felt a surge of unholy anger along with a flood of adrenaline. His rage blinded him. "You.... If anything—"

"Shut up and listen. Here's what you will do for us next."

9

____

O LD CHICAGO, WILLIANA

Sierra Blade acknowledged that the audience for her audio journal, *"Dark Light,"* was a niche, but large and growing. By invitation only, they doted on her every episode. The language of her show, while specialized, resonated with every listener. They were many.

"My name is Sierra. Unlike you and yours topside, you should know we need no *headlights* here in The Digs—our underground refuge. Because rays do not yet penetrate to the sub-basements, much less down to the upper tunnels.

"The lower tunnels provide additional protection, but most don't yet feel the need. Although each successive generation of high-power telecom microwaves will penetrate farther, nobody knows how far. Plus, lower tunnels are used for other purposes.

"Topside frogs ask, 'What's the big deal?'

"A bird like me would answer, 'Well, if you don't care about your organs getting microwaved, no matter where you are topside, no worries!'

"So we keep our headlights handy for ray checks each time they introduce new tech above. Crazy topsiders. You're not like them if you're listening right now. But what else can we do other than hide? Once they start spraying rays from clouds of satellites, though, nayers predict the end of days. If my mother gets her way. If you know me, you know who she is.

"Nayers—nihilistic naysayers—accept, even welcome, the logical conclusion of the frogs' destructive proclivities. Nayers not only embrace their own destruction, but everyone's. Without even realizing it. I ask you, why would God build this self-destructive tendency into the human genome if not as a cruel prank? *Does God laugh?*

"My headlight devices are two of my most precious possessions, along with my puters, my topside antenna and my repeater array. I need to stay informed of happenings up there. Even if others just ignore all that insanity, or just draw silly conclusions

"A warning: too many of you topside birds put too much confidence in your cages. Some of you feel what happens topside, or what those frog fools do or say up there doesn't much matter. I know better. Do you know better? *Birdman knows better.*

"Those of you who live in the open, in basements and even in sub-basements, may complain of symptoms. I took my headlights up there recently to discover the ray spray had grown worse since my last visit a few months earlier. I saw narrow green beams criss-cross up there like an intricate pile of iridescent pickup-sticks. Remember those? Like old-fashioned laser beams, but invisible without my headlight goggles, I could see some of those 10G beams passing right through the little people who camp up there." She paused at the memory, took a deep breath.

"After warning them they should seek safety in the lower levels, I bolted back down. Don't get me wrong. Copper fabric hoods and clothing helps. I even line my mask with stinky copper cloth.

"Some of you tweeners admit to living in fear, but will never complete your transition from topside like me. It's a decision. You, or someone you know, will live in a quasi-fugue state steeped in denial. Most tweeners ignore my warnings despite headaches and growths and sundry disorders such as confusion, depression, and disorientation Some can't keep food down, even when it's available. You probably know food is more scarce up there. They blame all their symptoms on malnutrition.

"The spray stains the homeless in large regionplexes the worst. Those with little or no metallic shielding are next. Some wear head cages made of silky copper fabric hoods and masks which slows their physical and mental devolution. But the smart ones, maybe like you, descend beneath earthen foundations and steel infrastructure. The day will come when metal rooms even in the lowest tunnels will be essential. Full-metal cages. Someday soon, if the topsiders get their way. Invisible beams will become lethal clouds. And they call *us* crazy! I remember shared moments with Birdman two years ago." For the benefit of her listeners, Sierra re-created a series of conversations she would never forget....

"WE LOOKED AT EACH OTHER. WE NEEDED NO WORDS. Birdman and I sat cross-legged, knee-to-knee, palms down. The oval rug on which we sat offered some insulation from the chilly floor planks. That rug was crafted of hand-braided strips of colored rags woven into ropes that were then coiled and sewn together.

Hey, B-man, where d'you get this radical retro rug?

His thoughts made me smile. '*Glad you like it, Sierra. I bartered some rutabagas grown in one of my deep-tunnel plots for it.*'

"I stared into his dark eyes by the light of a shimmering glow from a large candle snuggled into its stand on a low table at our elbows. The yellow flame wiggled as it danced to a slight draft that penetrated the ancient sill behind the table.

"Birdman experienced visions. Sometimes, he was an orphan in time. Without saying a word, he conveyed his wishes for a device that would become an essential survival tool. I saw it *with* him. These wordless moments of imperishable inspiration shared with the B-Man excited and horrified me. What a burden living with that curse... that gift. He thought, '*What defensive gear might help defend us more effectively from poisonous EM waves, Sierra?*'

"Focus shone on my youthful face, he had said. I remember I was so eager. If I hadn't known the B-man so well, those eyes of his might have frightened me. But I *did* know him. He was the father I never knew. He challenged me to leverage existing technology to create something new —what I would call *headlights*. I drew inspiration from a community of topside optical and neuronic engineers. Each possessed a piece of the puzzle.

"A few weeks later, Birdman and I met outside his apartment. Between his building and the one next door, we sat in an alley at a small wireframe table. I displayed my handiwork with pride by the light of several chem-globes suspended just overhead. *Well, sir, while this is a clunky prototype, it works. It renders harmful EM waves visible.* But I sensed my efforts fell short of the B-Man's vision.

"I continued, mentally conveying my meaning in a matter of milliseconds. *EM rays appear as green slivers to the wearer, and in more contaminated areas, they show up as clouds of various green hues. The deeper and more saturated the hue, the more harmful. The blue-green glow from within the device is an artifact of the headlight technology.*

"Birdman smiled, said nothing, but showered me with a wordless accolade. *'Sierra, that's brilliant!'* He gingerly handled the unwieldy device—a motorcycle flight helmet with an opaque shield in front of the wearer's eyes. Was he afraid he'd break it? He set it back on the table in front of him. His mind fell quiet.

"I explained the technology with a few focused ideas. Both of us stared at the device with tight lips, pondering its appearance. The entire affair looked both ancient and futuristic. All that subtly illuminated fiber-plasma circuitry embedded in copper & steel panels might have seemed stylish to a three centuries ago in the Victorian age. The thing was bulky, and heavy. I watched Birdman's face, scoured his mind. To the extent he allowed, anyway.

"Almost apologetically, I said out loud, 'I can miniaturize future versions with some nano stuff I scored from a salvager.' His eyebrows raised, creasing his forehead. I quickly added, 'We can also make it a lot less obvious and more comfortable.'

"He followed up with suggestive words of his own. His voice croaked from lack of use. 'Mmm... goggles, maybe?'

"'Um, yeah. Yeah! Why not? That'll take some time, B-Man.' Goggles made elegant sense. Otherwise, the wearer could become the subject of ridicule topside. Most frogs ignore the dangers of EM waves since they haven't yet connected it with various health issues, even though many suffer symptoms. Worse, they call us birds crazy conspiracy theorists which marginalizes our contribution to public welfare. Plus, some of you are painfully aware that those with unhelpful profit motives encourage this inflammatory rhetoric. A large device like this would fuel those flames any time we venture up and out.

" I remember thinking, *By donning our a simple pair of goggles, birds could walk among the non-believers. Ridicule from the frogs diminish by the day, anyway, as the science behind toxic EM pollution stabilizes and matures. And as frogs die.*

"That was two years ago. So much has changed, yet... not."

"I HAD TO CLOSE OFF FROM B-MAN'S DYSTOPIAN VISIONS OF the future and all that screeching noise. He understood. Poor B-Man. I prefer my cozy little tech world in The Digs. But now the visions are harder to turn off. They inspire me to create blueprints for other defensive measures—so I can sleep at night with a clear conscience knowing I've done all I am able.

"Over time, as ray-spray thickens, those of you close to the surface will come to use other defensive measures, short of going underground. Body cages—also called "lace"—enclose vital organs and appendages with metallic fabric.

The topside market for these products will increase once more birds and ex-frogs demand them, often after accepting the science and developing identifiable symptoms. Fear will spread. Even worse than... *normal.* Good.

"Even today, a few paranoid frogs, once viewed as delusional by more conservative frogs, use these devices in their everyday lives topside. Or they venture underground once they overcome their fear of committing to their convictions.

"One guarantee, my friends, things will get worse. Much worse. You need to know. My name is Sierra. Thanks for listening. "

10

N

EW WASH,
MARYGINIA

DUMB BELLS CLANKED, A CACOPHONY OF VOICES ECHOED OFF the hard walls. A jump rope snapped the floor rhythmically. Some gorilla pummeled a speed bag with a rapid *bump*-a-ta-*bump*-a-ta. And an occasional shout of encouragement punctuated the susurrus of the boxing club's background clatter.

Zaya French had dug into the two guys Joey K pointed out at the Fourth Street Gym. Neither appeared to be pillars of their communities. His homework revealed Mayfield Bailey—Mister Sucker Punch—was a telecom lobbyist on behalf of the Grandy Group who was courting Proconsul Libby Blade's favor. No secret there—public domain. The other guy, Anderson Dean, a supervisory agent with the Capitol Security Service, protected members of the Assembly. *Hmmm... 'Round 'n 'round.*

Like Joey K, Zaya saw Bailey and Dean at the gym at the same time. Joey said they always disassociated from one another. That was Zaya's impression too. Since he showed up at the gym at least five days each week, it was easy to notice such things. Sometimes one of these characters held the heavy bag for the other, or they just ended up in the free weight area at the same time. As a coincidence. Amateurs.

Dean always arrived at the gym with another big guy, but they'd separate just outside. That hulk would be his source since Dean remained unapproachable—too sharp and too paranoid. The big guy was over seven feet tall. Hired muscle. A thug. This Retif Zlatan worked for Dean at CSS. Zaya later learned this monster was born and raised in the region of Europe United they once called Bosnia. He migrated to the United Westicas in the forties after a lot of action. The many jagged scars on his forehead and both cheeks bore witness to a violent past, not to mention his hulking prowl.

Zaya passed close by the mountain of a man to start a conversation. The grizzled gorilla obviously made some assumptions based on Zaya's appearance, including several scars on his respectable biceps that were less tanned and more shiny than the rest of his arms. Zaya was no sun worshipper, not being suicidal, but was more dark-skinned than some. A sleeveless Road Commander t-shirt did nothing to hide any of that. Nor did his ratty boxing shorts. He looked like a fighter, despite his obvious maturity. So he guessed his well-crafted demeanor influenced the first tale this goon started blurting out after Zaya greeted him in the noisy free-weight area of the gym. Just two strangers engaged in idle banter while pumping iron.

Retif sat on a bench and curled a forty-pound dumbbell in his right hand with little effort. He spoke decent English but with a heavy accent and lousy grammar. Zaya under-stood him well enough to avoid making him angry from his perch on an obvious emotional precipice. He smiled. Rather, he leered at the opportunity for small talk with a non-threatening workout buddy. Told Zaya whenever he was driving a transport he was happy. Otherwise, not so much. But too many concussions made it difficult for him to keep his pilot's license. *Jeez.*

Then Retif shared a story he found humorous. Zaya listened hard to make sense of it because Retif thought his English was better than it was. He talked fast, almost as if he feared Zaya would disappear before he finished.

One day, he slugged a corrupt policy officer in the face. Odd this was the first anecdote he shared with a total stranger. "Before Westica, I work in river country at home. I stop for beer before getting on bus. Policyman tell me I must come with him. They do that. I say no. He pull my shirt on the long sleeve. I spin and hit him with my, ah, elbow? Like so. He fall down. He not moving." Retif smiled at the memory as he demonstrated the vicious blow before contin-uing. He stopped just inches from Zaya's left temple. Zaya flinched. He smiled. The big man was *quick.*

"I keep hitting and the kicking. I not know why. Others drag me off or Policyman would be dead now. It take many. Some would do same, but they not want trouble. I throw money at him on floor and walk to bus. I am late. I now live Westica, but go home sometimes. When I, ah, retire, ah, finish the work, I may go back there to stay. I miss to be myself. You know? You understand?"

Somewhat dumb-founded by this conversation, Zaya played along. "Yeah, I know. Sometimes it just feels good to hit something hard."

Desperate to change the subject, Zaya shrugged off this

incredible monologue and asked the big man about his work. An innocent question. But he got defensive. "I work for Alliance. Good job. Not all I think about, though. I have friends. Family too. But many things change. I change. Up here." He viciously banged his right temple with the blunt end of his sausage-size index finger while he struggled to release the dumb bell—a cramp in his other hand? Something else? Retif's massive forearms hid beneath bushes of curly black hair. Almost bald up top, Zaya wondered how many of those scars hid under a more youthful head of wiry hair a decade or three earlier.

Retif's formidable physique impressed Zaya, other than a sizable gut and after some serious miles, rode hard, and put away wet. That's what they used to say about four-legged beasts of burden called horses before their extinction. Retif fell silent with a small smirk, maybe recalling some other pleasant memory. Zaya made his escape from the thug's malevolent aura and from the odious combination of garlic and whiskey that hung on him in a pungent cloud. "Well, I better keep moving. Nice to meet you, Retif."

Met once again by that half-smile, half-leer, Zaya turned to leave, but heard a hoarse whisper trail off behind him. "I not have many friends. Many afraid to talk with Retif."

Seldom did Zaya both fear and pity someone. What memories and regrets this guy must harbor. One could only wonder what heinous acts Retif was asked—commanded— to perform for this Anderson Dean in his 'good Alliance job.'

11

N EW WASH, MARYGINIA

THE QUEEN PREENED ON HER THRONE. PROCONSUL LIBBY Blade from the great territory of Montanaho sat behind her nine-foot granite desk. Its glossy surface reflected the ceiling's indirect illumination. She surveyed her impressive office in the New Longworth Assembly Office Building on Independence Avenue south of the new Capitol, both located in New Wash. Much had been replicated on this side of the river from Old Washington as the water level had crept closer in recent years. As she observed her powdered, coifed and waxed image reflected in the glossy paneling to her right, she relished every detail of this office that shouted she was an influencial leader within the most powerful legislative body in the world. Libby knew who she was. She commanded all the attributes of power, and possessed an uncanny ability to wield her considerable personal wealth with great efficacy. They comprised her professional tool kit—her war chest.

One weakness—occasional appearances of her conscience—annoyed her. She knew right from wrong, and while she often reveled in the thrill of doing the wrong thing, she sometimes lost sleep over it. She treated that as if it were a gap in her defenses and an irritating character defect. But today, she would make monumental decisions and feel no remorse for their potential consequences. Days like today moved her forward. She became fearless.

While adding billions to her magisterial campaign's war chest, she would finalize support for launching her influence into outer space. Well, low Earth orbit, that is, Some suggested her actions might devastate humanity. Whatever they said did not matter. Not today. Because she believed the *science* was flawed, not her reasoning.

Today she would at last leverage the demise of her nemesis so many months ago, that self-righteous bitch, Mad Haley. No pity. No remorse. Not today.

Her bill on the floor for a vote this week would change everything:

Be it resolved...

Private and public enterprises shall be allowed to re-task public low-earth-orbit clusters of satellites known as CCS-11682 to CCS-79400, inclusive, and private clouds of satellites—herein collectively referred to as, "the cloud"—at their discretion for the economic welfare of their enterprises and commonly to benefit the citizens of the United Westican Territories, herein referred to as "the people."

Additional satellites and associated infrastructure may be added to the cloud with enterprise funding and public subsidies insofar as the needs of the enterprises and of the people are served."

The balance had tipped in her favor at last. Her staff reported the latest numbers. She was all but guaranteed success.

THE TRAIN WOULD NOT SERVE. PROCONSUL BLADE REFUSED TO ride one of the legislature's dedicated underground mag-lev cars north to the Capitol from her office in New Longworth. She buzzed her driver. By the time she reached her secure parking bay off Independence Avenue, her limousine awaited in a silent hover with the curbside portal sliding open as she approached.

The four-minute low-altitude ride up the hill to the east end of the Alliance Mall landed at the roof entrance of the Capitol. From there, her staff accompanied her on the short walk down to the Assembly Chambers while providing her updated numbers. By the time she finished her work today, votes in the Assembly of Elders for approval of AE8897 would be rubber stamps. But one must go through these motions. A few remained on the fence. She needed to look them in the eye to ensure they dropped to her side of that fence.

THEY WERE CLOSE. AE8897 OVERCAME ITS BIGGEST OBSTACLE with the death of a major opponent months earlier. Libby's own aide's treasonous activities also came to her attention. She discussed this with her chief of staff, Andrea Davies.

"Andy, are you sure Lucy's threats didn't hurt us?"

"Madame Proconsul, any potential fall-out from that

incident has been handled. Just like Secretary Haley. Any in opposition are receiving an unmistakable message."

"I don't like *handled*, Andy. Messy business."

"Well, you know better than most. Politics is always a hot sticky mess. But with what's at stake?"

"Yes, yes. Moving on, are all the telecoms still onboard?"

"They are loving you right now."

"Any more loose ends from the bill's oppo research?"

"None as far as we know. There is one thing, though. Our bots came across that nosy writer again… that *journalist*. Recall he publishes an audio journal every Thursday called *Redemption Alley*. He must have good sources. I pointed this out to you a week ago. We're keeping our eye on him for now. We'll escalate as required."

Madame Proconsul chose not to share with her chief of staff that outside help was also on the job. "Good. We don't need some journalist wannabe pissing in our soup, Andy."

"No, ma'am."

12

S CHAUMBURG,
WILLIANA

Being a thorough investigative journalist, Zaya French had reconstructed the final days of the murdered Secretary of Defense Madeleine Haley through accounts from her co-workers, colleagues, friends and family.

Madeleine bristled, hammer and tongs. She saw weaponized Social Media—the ultimate propaganda machine—now in the hands of enemies of the state. Billions of the lesser-informed leveraged SM as their primary source of information, yet SM was unfettered by any government oversight. Worse, traitors used it as an effective method to indoctrinate the masses—voters. This is where it all started.

Madame Secretary mustered the personal courage to become a political and societal pariah to do something about this. As a cabinet member, she appealed to the leader of the Alliance—Madame Magister—and the rest of her cabinet to treat weaponized SM as a clear and present danger to the Alliance, and even to global security. This was nothing short of information warfare.

Anybody who wished to protect their political capital, however, steered clear of what they considered a fool's errand. They asserted nobody possessed the power to effect such sweeping societal changes, at least no politician. Then, a century ago, entire governments toppled after enacting legislative restrictions on SM platforms called Facebook, Twitter and others. It was called *the will of the people*. But Haley discovered the real reason for so much resistance to her quest. And that reason eclipsed her original concerns. She realized she would not survive. Two years into her tenure, already a pariah from her war against SM and other existential threats to which nobody else paid any attention, someone murdered her.

During her deep dive into satellite-enabled SM technology, she got wind of an audacious telecommunications consortium aggressively supporting a mission called TESS —Targeted Exposure from Surveillance Satellites. TESS was not a concept meant for public consumption, nor even for hers. Privatized satellites would perform personal surveillance, plus an even more nefarious mission known only to a select few. This TESS technology further enabled Grandy Group's TEMP strategy—Targeted ElectroMagnetic Poisoning. They could selectively disorient human and animal targets from space, or in more extreme cases, create physical maladies anywhere on the globe achieved with focused bursts of intense EM energy. They could even assassinate individual or group targets from space. All without government oversight. *And* they could made such deaths seem like natural expiries days or weeks after a massive and sudden exposure to a lethal dose of EMP.

Their platform would be eleventh generation (11G) telecommunications technology. The current 10G technology set the stage, ostensibly all for the sake of better and faster voxcons, vidcons, vidcords, 3D holograms and *fast* access to all feeds, anywhere, from any compatible device.

Huge conglomerates would profit by weaponizing mood control and even cancer grenades shot from global ray guns orbiting in space. Even if this bold strategy leaked, nobody would believe such outrageous capabilities could exist. Well, almost nobody. In order for this strategy to be effective, its proponents believed they must hide behind a mask of absolute innocence and secrecy.

Both TESS and TEMP horrified Madeleine Haley. Even as her initial postulations were viewed with skepticism by United Westican intelligence agencies, she lobbied a few influential Elders, including the indefatigable ProConsul of the Assembly. But before she could act further, while visiting her daughter in the Western Chicago neighborhood of Schaumburg, someone abducted, tortured and vivisected Madame Secretary Haley.

Message sent and delivered.

13

———

NEW WASH,
MARYGINIA

———

ZAYA SAT WITH FATHER LAMATTE FOLIÉRE IN THE COCKPIT OF his transport parked in the Restful Acres RV Resort in the western New Wash exurbs. Now just Lamatte Foliére, he had become Zaya's unlikely ally and was trying both to protect his friend, Sister Maria, and to reconcile his actions with his faith. He had shed his robes for now, and perhaps his vows. Lamatte was now just a conflicted guy in blue jeans, a sweatshirt and boots.

Zaya concealed the transport's steering controls with a pinching gesture near a dash sensor as he swiveled his pilot's seat to face Lamatte who sat in the seldom-occupied co-pilot's seat near the entry portal. They sat almost knee-to-knee in the small cockpit with warm lighting in marked contrast to the cool conspiratorial tone of Zaya's voice. This was serious. He needed backup.

"Look, Lamatte, you know I've been investigating a series of murders disguised as accidents or suicides. Someone is tying up loose ends in covering up a plan to legislate global electromagnetic poisoning. At least, that is my strong belief."

"Really? *That* sounds like a stretch. Don't you think you're just paranoid?" He squirmed in his seat looking more nervous than Zaya would have suspected.

Zaya said, "Damn right. If something happens to me, I need someone to continue telling the story."

"You're serious, aren't you? Zaya, you're scaring me."

"Promise me, Lamatte."

"Ah, well, I'll do what I can, but I will *not* put Maria in further danger. Best I can offer." Lamatte rose to his feet and prepared to catch a train back to St. Vroman's Rectory. Curious that he suddenly seemed so anxious to leave.

"Good enough for now, my friend."

ALONE FIVE MINUTES LATER, ZAYA THOUGHT, *WHY DO I PUNISH myself asking questions for which I can find no answers. What will be the implications of sustained and high-power levels of global electromagnetic radiation? And in the context of all the other atrocities we done to the planet? Who can say with any certainty?*

EMP had been a longstanding threat. And soon, by passing AE8897—Proconsul Libby Blade's power play—the threat was about to get *much* worse. He knew unscrupulous players had greased the right palms with mountains of money, and silenced sundry whistle blowers. The turbid forces of power and greed had orchestrated this dance of slow death. Or maybe not so slow. With years of commercial groundwork in place, enabled by low-profile privatized launches, thousands of *communication* satellites would be re-purposed to become potential weapons mere months after 8897 became policy. And their control would rest in the hands of an avaricious few.

But there was a price. They would effectively place the population of Planet Earth inside a microwave oven. Even as air has become scarce and water toxic.

They discredit those who pay attention and speak out as "conspiracy nuts." The pejorative label given to these alleged lunatics? *Birds.* In the past, the rhetoric of a greedy few to inspire blind obedience labeled such critical thinkers *snowflakes.* .

Zaya grinned. *Let the blizzard begin!*

14

NEW WASH, MARYGINIA

ZAYA SAT IN SOLITUDE HOURS AFTER LAMATTE LEFT. THE gentle glow of indicator lights in his transport reminded him that countless systems provided him comfort and safety. When they worked. He silently thanked his alarm and air filtration systems, not to mention his whole-house oxygen trickler. Various information detection and acquisition systems ran non-stop on his puters as background bots scoured all the major feeds.

He was perplexed. Lamatte Foliére had spoken ominous words on the lev platform in the exurbs of New Wash, "You had no right to write about my relationship with Grandy. Now I'm a dead man." Those words bothered Zaya. *Grandy Group uses assassins? Or were the priest's words hyperbole?*

Grandy was huge—one of the world's largest media conglomerates. What might get Foliére killed by having his relationship with them revealed? And in an obscure streaming broadcast like *The Alley*, no less? Grandy was everywhere. But *there*? Zaya reveled in perverted delight that his work could have such an impact. His weary mind refused to shake the thought. There would be no letting go now. Sometimes he took intense pleasure envisioning himself more than a simple storyteller, as an investigative journalist who could make a real difference in a house-of-cards world—an insipid dream of someone who lost his higher purpose once upon a time.

There was no doubt Father Foliére's fears called for vigilance. And at that precise moment, Zaya heard the disturbance outside his bus, his home. Innocent visitors do not drop by unannounced a few minutes before midnight. He grabbed a claw hammer and a body spot. Clipped the spot to his tunic's collar. He'd risk leaving his mask inside for a quick peek outside. Not sure he'd be able to use this hammer, this—this weapon—on another human being. He shivered at the thought. But survival instincts were compelling.

As backup before he ventured out, Zaya swiped his hand in front of the proximity pad on an overhead panel in the cockpit to light up the bus's exterior. The number one deterrent against intruders? Light 'em up. The number two deterrent? A debilitating sound wave from his security system's 160 dB siren. No need for that. Yet. Besides, he could activate that outside from his WristPad, if necessary.

Zaya gestured *Open Portal* by clamping his thumb and index finger near the pad and then spread them apart. The portal swished open and thumped against its forward stops harder than normal. He made a mental note to re-level the bus in the morning. Auto-level was broken. A few of the jacks must've settled into the dirt below. Again. He strangled the hammer's handle in his right hand. The hands-free spot clipped to his upper chest paled in the ocean of light hurled outward by the plasmas and strips on the bus. This impressive array of illumination only added to the hazy ambience of New Wash skyline and the air around him. Zaya already regretted leaving his mask inside, huffing to breathe.

Like high-beams in a blizzard, something just beyond the lights signaled an uninvited visitor to this neglected campground at New Wash's semi-rural periphery, but remained unseen. Modular housing cubicles clustered around his bus. They looked like old shipping containers painted with primary colors, now faded to translucent pastels. Between and around them, weeds dominated the once-elaborate landscaping in the park.

Most amusing to Zaya came an unbidden thought as he scanned an array of dilapidated mag-pull trailers in the diluted shadows. Even while flirting with an intruder, he played with words. He mentally sketched a scene in his mind's eye for one of his works in progress. What if gravity quit working? Would these tenacious weeds still anchor most everything to the ground?

A sagging chain-link fence topped with tired razor wire surrounded this thirty-site low-rent neighborhood. Yet the proprietor had the temerity to call the place a *resort*." Hysterical. Why did that gnaw at me? Zaya would soon need to get back inside to a decent O2 trickle. Silly thoughts. Fifteen yards northwest of his rig, faded yellow construction tape surrounded a small pond pretending to be a swimming pool. He guessed that dingy pit hadn't seen water in decades. Looked more like a crime scene.

Two crude benches with sagging backs crouched along the edge of a shuffleboard court to his north. White lines and numbers long ago surrendered to weed-filled cracks.

Nothing there, either. Fallen leaves from the few stunted trees, bits of trash, and other detritus of dense human habitation littered both sides of the narrow and neglected roads. Along the base of the rusty perimeter fence ten yards to his east, piles of trash accumulated. To Zaya's south, strewn between trailers, rusty transport carcasses filled the gaps between a few still-occupied trailers of various colors. He knew they were old because they no longer used steel to build such vehicles. For a few decades now. Only old steel rusts like that.

And then there was Stan's double-wide, the memory of which haunted him.

WHEN ZAYA HAD PAID IN ADVANCE FOR HIS SITE RENTAL FOR the month, he remembered he regretted knocking on the portal of the old man's shack. A desiccated handi-ramp with a crumbling railing fronted the decrepit doublewide cube. Stan, the camp host, had cracked open his front portal. Its once-white frame was filthy with prints and unidentifiable gray-brown streaks. Zaya remembered being repulsed by toxic waves of ammonia. He suspected the elderly vagabond was the campground's owner as well as its host, but would not admit to that. Twenty cats inside might have been a conservative estimate. Stan's most pronounced features protruding from the shadows were his immense gut and deformed fingers clamping that dirty portal's frame in a white-knuckled death grip. A memorable old sot—stubbled, nervous, malodorous.

As Zaya snapped out of that grim recollection, the hammer grew heavier in his hand. He focused once again on the intruder, imagining that tool colliding with flesh and bone. He shivered. At that moment, with lungs now craving O2, and a bout of dizziness coming on strong, he wheeled around to meet the approaching threat that was more imposing than a large feral dog—the biggest raccoon he'd ever seen. The beast lumbered past offering Zaya only the slightest sideways glance. Had to be a mutation. It skirted this bothersome human presence around one of the shuffle-board benches. The critter emanated a waft of an adventurous odor as it bumped a trash receptacle that tipped on its side with a noisy clatter. Zaya's overwhelming sense of relief almost trumped his shock at this unexpected turn of events. Once more, he had fallen prey to his prolific imagination. With adrenaline still roiling, he envisioned how he might leverage this scene somewhere in his work. The life of a writer.

Zaya needed some perspective. But he had also better be realistic. The real threat hadn't yet materialized. Didn't mean it wouldn't. Worsening dizziness and the genesis of a headache now compelled him to seek O2 fast.

That night he slept hugging that hammer after scribbling dozens of pages in an actual-paper notebook. Old-school. He always needed fodder for the literary cannon, even with potential risk never far away.

15

———

NEW WASH, MARYGINIA

———

ZAYA'S HEAD BUZZED WITH A MELANGE OF CONCERNS. Electromagnetic pollution—or *poisoning*, if you weren't in denial—had become such a controversial subject, one of the more dangerous dimensions of climate change. Birds, the believers, did whatever they could to protect themselves *and* to spread the science to frogs, the disbelievers.

Mayfield Bailey, a lobbyist who worked out at the Fourth Street gym, just *had* to be a crucial connection. Grandy Group, the world's largest telecom conglomerate, purchased an influential member of the Assembly for her support and leadership. Then, that Assemblywoman's aide learned of this through her research at Georgetown University in the reading room where Father Foliére volunteers. She clearly had planned to go public, working with a climatologist, later murdered, for his scientific credibility. Then *she* overdosed and died.

Now, the darkness in the ramshackle RV park pressed in, eery with the incessant but quiet humming of invisible traffic close overhead. Lights in the skyways were forbidden. Zaya forgot why. But the susurrus of their swift passage in the darkness provided another reminder why he hated the exurbs of sprawling regionplexes like New Wash. Had the dull night sky allowed visibility to the stars, their rapid blinking in and out would have announced ghostly silhouettes rushing overhead. But nobody had seen stars for at least a decade.

An alarm chirped like a psychopathic parakeet. Zaya jumped as if that parakeet pecked the back of his neck with its razor-sharp little beak. Spotted Lamatte on the security vid after he penetrated the bus's scan zone. Seconds later, the priest knocked. Zaya swished open the portal. After a brief pause, and with concern, he said, "How d'you find me, Father?"

"That's not important." He mumbled some nonsense about his psychic-friend-finder ability. "It's just Lamatte now. I am no longer a priest. I need your help."

That grabbed my attention. "Come in. Please." Zaya recalled the altercation on the lev train platform just a week ago where the priest had pulled a gun, threatening to shoot him in the back. But then their most recent conversation, he had promised to tell Zaya's story should anything happen. Friends didn't come easily to Zaya, and when they did, he wouldn't turn them away. Lamatte climbed the five steps instead of using the lift. Zaya watched his body language. No sign of disguised hostility. Instead, once he'd removed his mask, what Zaya saw underneath, besides common mask rash, seemed more like despair, or defeat. But most of all, he saw apprehension.

"Sit. How can I help?" Zaya remained standing, arms crossed while Lamatte dropped heavily into the co-pilot's seat.

"Look, Zaya, I have nowhere to turn. Ever since you wrote that story about me and Grandy, I've known my life is over. But let me assure you, it's not your fault. I lashed out, from guilt. For that, I am sorry."

"Lamatte, I still don't understand what you're getting at. I interviewed you at Georgetown about a young lady—"

"Lucy."

"Yes. Lucy frequented your reading room. I discovered who she was, dug deeper, and found something disturbing. And your description of the contents of her journal you later shared with me? Explosive."

"Yes, and two days later they killed her. That was no overdose. Like the other suspicious deaths you said you're looking at. Neither accidents nor suicides."

Zaya's eyes went wide. Scratched his chin, jutted his jaw. "*I* know. But how do *you* know.... Lamatte? Isn't it time we level with each other?" He observed Lamatte's dark features, his thick black hair matted against a squarish forehead as if he'd strolled in from the rain. It hadn't rained for hours. He remained a striking figure. Odd that he'd worn neither hat nor hood.

"Fair enough. I sense you're a good man on a worthy quest."

"You sense? Like intuition? Wait, what? A quest? How—"

"Zaya, I sense things much as others see or hear things. In fact, that's what I wish to speak with you about. As you already know, Lucy found out what her boss in the

Assembly was conspiring, and with whom. That earned her a coffin. You're next."

Now, Zaya both wanted him to slow down and to speed up. This could confirm his research and suspicions. His patience had worn thin. He turned to squarely face the ex-priest, hands on his knees, leaned forward. "Tell me what you know, Lamatte. Right now."

"I screwed up. I fell in love."

This was not at all what Zaya expected to hear.

A DAM BURST. LAMATTE TOO LEANED FORWARD, HEAD DOWN, his hands folded as if he were praying to his still-shiny shoes. His confession confirmed what Zaya already knew. Lamatte's words now gushed like swollen flood waters riddled with floating debris. He rushed to get them out while he still mustered the courage to do so, but snagged on his conflicting emotions. He could not look anywhere but at those shoes. "I'm being blackmailed into performing unspeakable acts, Zaya. That cost me my faith, and maybe my love. Lucy dug deep after learning her boss, the Proconsul of the Assembly, accepted huge campaign contributions—dark money—from three media conglomerates. A cabal. The largest of those, by far, is Grandy. Someone there must have received an alert when Lucy accessed classified documents from one of the library's puters. That sent them in my direction. She was terrified by what she learned. I picked up on that. In fact, I received such strong impressions from her it made me ill for a time. Then we talked. When two thugs came to the library, I panicked. I was *so* obvious. They questioned me. Somehow, they knew everything about me. About my past, and my relationship with Maria... Sister Maria. Do you see?"

Zaya's frustration grew. "What were you told to do, Lamatte?"

"Don't you understand? They *interrogated* me. I told them *everything*. I told them Lucy discovered the deal her boss made with Grandy and the others. In return, she would spearhead favorable legislation and bury any resistance to their agenda."

"What agenda?"

"Doesn't matter right now. There's no time. I was to call a number the next time Lucy showed up at the library, or they would kill my precious Maria. I did, *and they killed Lucy*. Oh, God, what have I done! And now I've led them to you. Zaya, I had no choice. You understand, don't you?"

"What?" Zaya rocketed to his feet. His eyes darted to his security monitors on instinct. "Foliére, what in Hell have you done now?"

"They continue to tie up loose ends, Zaya. At first, I didn't think they'd use my insights to decimate all threats to their plot. An energy guy, a climatologist, a whistle-blower at Grandy, others Lucy discovered... but you know all that. And now *you* are getting too close, putting it all together, very publicly. I wanted to warn you. I *needed* to warn you. What did you expect, Zaya? You're broadcasting it all." They both fidgeted with fury. "A two-man team will move in as soon as I leave. They believe I'm still of use to them. They're wrong. I'll disappear, with your help."

"You son-of-a-bitch! You set me up?"

Now Lamatte spoke with an even greater urgency, as if time had run out. "Don't you see? If I don't do this, Maria dies. And they find you, anyway. This way.... But don't worry. You will survive. Probably." Lamatte shoved a small device toward Zaya. "Here. Take this pulser." He pressed it into Zaya's right hand. The nasty little device looked like obese brass knuckles. "Within moments after I leave, the first will knock. They know how to avoid your cams. You're supposed to think I'm returning. After disabling you, the second guy waiting at the front of your transport will help restrain you, put you inside, and start a fire. Another accident. These thugs are formidable, Zaya, but so are you, and you now command the element of surprise. Disable the first. This device's shock function will knock him out for hours. Then you disable the second. After that, you and I will disappear. We'll go to Chicago. You need to visit an old friend."

All Zaya could say was, "What? Jeez, Lamatte!" The erstwhile priest got up and left without another word.

THIRTY SECONDS AFTER THE PORTAL CLOSED BEHIND LAMATTE, the expected knock on the portal still startled Zaya. The cams had gone dark. Gripping the pulse weapon in front of him—set to render unconscious, not to kill—Zaya steadied himself with two deep breaths. While he was no stranger to weapons of violence, he hated them. But this was about survival. Is it not ironic how rigid ethics soften once hard danger thunders in?

Zaya shouted through the closed portal, standing off to the side. "What did you forget, Lamatte?" A distraction. After signaling to the prox panel with a quick *Open Portal* gesture, it swished open fast and hard. At that same instant, Zaya fired the weapon down into his first would-be attacker's face.

Before bad guy number one had even toppled backwards, Zaya force-fell onto him, still in bare feet. They tumbled to the weedy ground in a heap. Zaya made sure he landed on top and rolled to his right in one smooth motion. Faced the front of the transport with the gun gripped in his dominant left hand. As soon as the silhouette appeared around the corner of the bus, Zaya fired across his chest. Number two went down. Hard. And silent. Except for the soprano static from the little pulser.

Lamatte appeared from around the adjacent trailer. "I knew you'd be okay, Zaya. They should be unconscious for a few hours."

"Here. Take this damn thing. Doesn't make much noise, does it? Like a skinny bolt of baby lightning. Let's stow these gentlemen somewhere discreet. Give me a hand. We'll drag them behind old Stan's double-wide over there. With the other trash on the heap. They'll wake up and leave before he notices anything."

16

S T. VROMAN'S RECTORY
NEW WASH,
MARYGINIA

HOLLOW ECHOES OF THE LARGE HALL REVERBERATED THE sound of approaching footsteps. Father Benedict Scolario's voice dripped with disdain. "You! What are you doing back here, *Father*? You abandoned your *vows* long ago, did you not? I see you've abandoned your cassock. Have you left something behind, Foliére?"

Though Lamatte had not planned to engage this vexatious husk of a man, Father Scolario offered such a compelling invitation. "Bless you, Father Benedict, for reminding me I've violated my vows with my profound love for Maria. And for an affection denied you because of your own vows. The last time I graced this hall my focus was on Maria. But your presence hiding in this very hall, eavesdropping—with evil thoughts—did not escape my attention."

At that, Father Benedict Scolario lurched.

"Yes, your *thoughts*, Father." Now it was Lamatte's voice that dripped with disdain. "Weeks ago, I confessed to you my relationship with Sister Maria, and my conversations with Proconsul Blade's aide, along with my concern for her safety. I'm sure His Holiness, Bishop Giovanni, supports your violation of the most sacred seal of the confessional. I also know you revealed my conversations with Lucy Candelson to that abomination Carmen Rios at Grandy. He blackmailed me based on *your* actions, and he had Lucy *murdered*." Lamatte's voice wavered, but did not break.

Father Benedict made every attempt to appear un-afflicted by Lamatte's scathing indictment. But he was consumed by his own pious hatred for the pretender who stood before him mumbling nonsense. But then Lamatte's next words sank in, and Benedict's face began to melt. "*Is His Holiness aware of these violations of your most sacred vows, Father? That your actions resulted in the violent death of one of God's children? Father Benedict? No? Well, perhaps I should make a voxcon of my own."*

Lamatte was careful to keep his tone low and even, containing as little malice as possible toward this contemptible human being. He planned to disengage at that point. But.... "Well, please consider confessing *your* sins, Father. Perhaps you'll feel better. But choose your confessor with more care than I. You were the only person who knew of my relationship with Lucy, *and* with Maria. After I was foolish enough to trust you, I was also foolish to submit to Rios and to his vile threats. I must live with that for all my days."

Now flustered, Father Benedict's entire face flushed scarlet enough to match the gin bloom on his cheeks and on that bulbous nose adorned with a magnificent spider web of purple veins. After a long staring silence, Father Benedict said, "You young fool, I did no such thing!"

"Well, I will share a little secret with you, Father. My faith in you no longer blinds me. I can read your thoughts easier than I hear your words, thanks to one of the Lord's mysterious gifts. Unlike your sanctimonious lips, your wretched mind can no longer deceive me. Oh, and out of respect for our hard-working sisters who do your laundry, stop masturbating on your sheets, for goodness' sake. Good day, Father."

Lamatte held his gaze in a vice-like grip. Benedict Scolario's jaw dropped, his left eye twitched, and his rope-like lips knotted into an uncertain grimace. He grunted, turned with his imperious robes billowing and stumped off, issuing what might have been a whimper of submission.

Instead of thinking, *Good day*, Lamatte thought, *Good riddance.* He'd seek forgiveness later.

17
———

Chicago, Williana

Lamatte and Zaya traveled to Chicago to interview Captain Judge Miners of the Chicago Enforcement Department. *And* to escape local assassins. Zaya wanted to catch up with his old friend, Detective Lionel Smith, who said he worked for *Captain Drop-Dead-Gorgeous* at the CED. That was when meeting Smitty's boss became a moral imperative. Besides, Lamatte convinced him that visit would be key to his investigation.

A twenty-minute hyper-lev flight whisked them from Baltimore-Philly International to one of the six lev craft platforms atop Obama Tower, Chicago's tallest building. The quiet time in the cozy but comfortable cabin gave them a chance to compare notes. They sat shoulder-to-shoulder.

Zaya updated Lamatte on his entire investigation. Lamatte expanded on the story he shared with Zaya just before the attack at his transport, including who held the leash on that pair of would-be assassins. Zaya had assumed they were Grandy muscle. He was wrong. Lamatte told him of a conversation he overheard en route to the attack. They reported to their boss. They were contractors for a company called the Security Service. He heard the dispatcher also call them SS.

Upon landing, they caught a lev that carried them to the surface two hundred floors below the platform in less than sixty seconds. Zaya loved vertical acceleration, but thought Lamatte might puke. Why did that please him, just a little? At an altitude of twenty meters, the same taxi took them to the two-hundred-fifty-sixth precinct house of the CED. Four minutes later, they slipped into a parking structure on the sixth floor through a street-side bay. Walked the fifty yards to screening walls inside the precinct house barricade. Its scanners made their skin tingle.

The desk admin assigned them an escort to Captain Miners' platform. Since they voxconned their ETA on the way over from the O Tower, they were expected. Waiting in her outer office, they could see through the wall that Smitty's very blonde captain's puter and a voxcon commanded her full attention. She repeatedly blew her long bangs away from her eyes. Adorable.

Zaya idly wondered, *Why would she even talk with me? Because I was Smitty's old buddy? Or because I might help her solve SecDef's cold-case homicide? Sorry, Lamatte... so **we** could help solve the Haley case.*

Lamatte smiled.

During a voxcon earlier in the day, Smitty reminded Zaya that one of their beat cops had interviewed a group of witnesses—birds—when they canvassed the neighborhood surrounding the scene the day the body was discovered.

Now *that* got Zaya's attention. Smitty couldn't know one of his secret passions included learning as much as possible about the bird sub-culture. Talking with them could further Zaya's investigation. After setting the stage with his captain, Smitty invited the two travelers in with a huge smile on his somewhat pudgy face.

"ZAYA! YOU FIREPLUG! WELCOME TO THE TWO-FIVE-SIX. Damn, how is it you stay so tan? Not that fake micro-tat shit, is it?"

"Smitty! You forget I'm half injun, half *eye-talian?* Man, you got, ah, *rotund*, dude. Wanna hit the gym with me while I'm here? Pump some iron? *Or* I know this Lakota chief up near Hayward, if he's still alive. Has a sweat lodge next to the coldest lake in Williana." Lamatte and the captain watched the back-slapping man-hugging ritual with amusement after which Smitty and Zaya offered them embarrassed shrugs 'n smirks. Smitty introduced his captain with obvious deference after a look at Zaya that said, *Yeah, she is a force to be reckoned with, but she's also a good shit.* And she *was* drop-dead-gorgeous.

"Captain, Zaya French here is not just a minor celebrity broadcaster—"

Zaya feigned insult. "*Minor?*"

Smitty smiled at the interruption "—he's also a serious investigative journalist. He knows how to keep his mouth shut when off the record. Tells me his partner here, Father Lamatte Foliére, is his consultant."

Lamatte said, "Well, it's just Lamatte, and we play off each others' strengths."

Captain Miners was courteous, but Zaya watched her squint eyes with a slantways glance, like she was analyzing a witness's credibility. "Nice to meet you gents. Smitty tells me he believes you can bring value to our Haley case. Otherwise, you would not be here. Are we as one, guys?"

Zaya said, "We are, Captain. So what say we get to work?"

"Well said, Mr. French. May I call you Zaya? Good. So what can you do for me?"

Once Zaya laid out his entire investigation spanning more than a year of digging, her eyebrows crept ever higher. Toward her natural white-blonde bangs atop the highest and sharpest cheekbones he'd ever seen, he found her huge smokey green eyes captivating. After he finished, with Lamatte having augmented the presentation at several points, Zaya asked to review the on-scene witness statements. Smitty said, "One of the birds, a young girl, heard two things from two different voices: 'She oughta be pleased,' and 'Rudest job for SS yet.'"

Zaya said, "Interesting. Now here's a new nugget. Lamatte?"

"Captain, the two-man team sent to silence Zaya in New Wash just before we came out here worked for the Security Service. They're a contractor whose primary client is the United Westican Territories Assembly of Elders. They're sometimes called by their historical name—the Capitol Security Service."

"Holy shit! *SS!*"

Zaya said, "Captain, a key element of my entire investigation revolves around EMP. The latest major legislation to turn the corner for the big three telecoms is before the Assembly. Soon it goes to the floor for a vote. It's called

AE8897. The primary advocate for that bill is the Assembly of Elders' Proconsul*woman* Libby Blade."

"Oh, now wait, Zaya. That's thin. We'd better have more than that."

"Yes, we had better. Now, Captain, this will stretch our credibility with you, but it's necessary. Lamatte here possesses a strong sense of, well, intuition. He senses things and reads people better than anyone I know. We're asking your permission to partner with Smitty in a search for your witnesses and ask them more questions."

"We've searched."

"I'm sure you have. We bring different skills to bear, given the chance, regardless of whether this stuff floats your boat, or not. What do you have to lose? And what to gain if Lamatte digs out more intel?"

"Wow. Um, well, sure. Why not? I am under so freaking much pressure for progress on Secretary Haley's murder, so I'm considering every option. I'll grasp at whatever straw you're offering. We're getting lots of help, you can imagine, but so far, nothing. I'll expect you to report everything you discover to me, and only to me. You don't tell anyone what methods you're using. Agreed?"

"Thank you, Captain."

"So eight AM, meet back here. We'll get you started. We need evidence."

Lamatte said, "No offense, Captain, but we should start now, even though my favorite time of day approaches —dinnertime."

"Well, you're the consultant. Informant. Whatever. It'll be dark soon, if that matters."

18

———

OLD CHICAGO,
WILLIANA

———

SWEAT DRIPPED FROM THE TIP OF SMITTY'S AQUILINE NOSE.
He wasn't fat, just a bulky street warrior clad in armor that
appeared remarkably similar to an excess of adipose tissue.
The trio had hiked a quarter-mile from their unmarked
CED transport parked on Lakeshore, conspicuous by its lack
of adornment and a flat-black finish. Still farther to go. Smitty's was thirsty, and his mask helped, but he still grew dizzy
and sensed the genesis of a headache. He upped his O2
trickle. Last thing he needed was dehydration *and* hypoxia.

———

THE STREETS GREW DARK AND NARROW, TRANSITIONING FROM
plasticrete to ancient macadam in acute disrepair. Smitty
said, "So you got a *gift,* Lamatte? What's that mean?"

Zaya hoisted a crooked smiled, like he knew what was coming. Lamatte winked at him, unobserved by Chicago's finest.

They moved through the urban jungle like a trio of respectable alley cats with Smitty leading the way through the emerging dusk. Despite the poor illumination from light posts leaning like drunken sailors, Smitty's skepticism lit up his face with a curious asymmetry. Underneath his Akubra —a wide, floppy-brimmed hat with a dented crown—Smitty reminded Lamatte of the fictional film figure Van Helsing, a notorious vampire hunter of olde. Beneath that chapeau now cocked back in the clammy but chilly twilight, Lamatte observed wrinkles that sculpted Smitty's pasty forehead above his CED-issued mask. "Well, Smitty, gift or curse, it's like strong intuition backed by a crazy keenness to emotions I feel coming off people in waves. Much like a very sensitive nose might pick up on moods from someone's odor. Not too controllable, but sometimes it throws impressions at me. Remember, you asked.

"Take you, for example," Lamatte said, as he kept his eyes straight ahead as they trudged through the abandoned streets, now alongside the aging cop, "I sense you're a good friend to most everyone you meet, at least to those on the right side of the law. But you and Zaya share something special even though you haven't seen each other in years. Did one of you save the other's life back in the day? Under somewhat embarrassing circumstances? You worry your wife will think you're fat, Smitty. You love her so much and don't want to lose her. You're also in love with Captain Miners. Not that you've ever told anyone because it's a source of personal embarrassment. You're petrified she'll find out and send you away. You are a superb detective, and you're embarrassed about that too. No need. You have lots of folks who look up to you, Smitty." Lamatte's eyes widened as he swiveled his to catch Smitty's. "Oh my, did you know your cholesterol is off the bloody charts? Ought to get checked out. How far off am I? Just impressions, you understand."

"Lamatte, *shut up*, man. Alright, already! Jeez!"

Zaya chuckled and said, "Fucks with your mind, don't it, ole buddy?"

"God! Okay, you got skills. Crap! You are *scary*, man."

"Yeah, I get that sometimes. Like when I open my big mouth to show off. No offense. Are we getting close, Smitty?" Lamatte was mad at himself. Showing off was stupid. His knees felt rubbery. He remembered the old adage, "ain't nothin' for nothin'."

LIONEL SMITH, DECORATED DETECTIVE. YET HE STILL WORKED to recover from creepy wonder. He was a good cop because he believed his five senses. Now this sixth-sense crap threw him into a mental mud storm. But his good cop sense—his own sixth sense—allowed him to recover faster than most. So be it. Evidence. Of a most personal nature. Once again all business, he said, "We're seven blocks off Lakeshore, an older part of the city. Lots of tunnels beneath old buildings built on top of older foundations. The connecting tunnels are an impossible maze that meander many levels below the basements in this area. At least four or five levels, maybe more. Here in the Midwest, winters can be brutal. Lots of inside spaces, like old walking subways, train tunnels and hubs from the old days. They spared folks from going outside. Always been that way. We don't go down there much any more, and then only one or two levels below the basements. And we never do so without 3D trackers that leave digital bread crumbs so we can backtrack."

"Who lives down there?"

"Well, nobody knows. Sometimes we sweep the upper-level tunnels below buildings still occupied because everyone we meet are squatters and trespassers by definition. But it's like pissing up a flagpole. And considering how little evidence we find of other crimes, it's only a token effort."

Lamatte said, "Has it always been like this?"

Smitty said, "Well, when the statehood-to-territory merger passed into policy in the thirties, the Alliance was formed as a perceived political necessity. Uncertainty drove unprecedented migration around that time. The combined states of Wisconsin, Illinois, and Indiana now comprised the territory known as Williana within the then-new Alliance called the United Westican Territories. So yes, at least since then."

Ever the well-researched reporter, Zaya said, "Statistics show that the greater Chicago regionplex spanning the old Indianapolis-Chicago-Madison geographical area boasts a larger homeless population than most, which is surprising considering the bitter temps up here compared to the southern plexes."

Smitty said, "Sounds right. We've come across entire communities down there from all over. Some seem self-sufficient. But those we encounter often move after we leave. Farther down? Dunno. Some respect the badge, some don't. Here we are—where the officer interviewed the witnesses."

THEY CROSSED MICHIGAN, A NARROW SIDE STREET, AND stopped in front of a boring three-story red brick building well past its prime—a store once. An unlocked portal allowed them entry. Most windows were intact. That surprised Zaya. Before they entered, he noticed several boarded windows on the upper floors that lent the building a tired look, but not dead.

As they stood in the store with little to look at other than dusty debris on the floor, their pale shadows faded in the late-autumn dusk. Since the dingy edifice faced northeast, they already stood in a murky twilight. The instinct to light up this musty old room tugged at them all. Smitty swept aside his waistcoat and reached into a voluminous cargo pocket of his tactical pants. In a gentle voice, Lamatte said, "Guys, someone's here, behind that wall about fifteen feet ahead. Two or three. I suggest no spots for now."

Smitty amused Zaya. He accepted Lamatte's prognostication as factual and stopped reaching for his powerful cop spot. That thing would light up this joint like high noon on a sunny Lakeshore day of fifty years ago.

In a conciliatory tone, Smitty said softly, "Policy officer. Please come out. No problem. We'd just like to talk for a sec, okay?"

Lamatte added, "And no need for any alarms, eh? We're here for a simple followup on the murder of that poor lady near here a while back."

They stood there. For almost a minute. They thought they heard a muted discussion. First, one slight man who appeared well-nourished, if not clean-shaven, stepped out with obvious trepidation. His face remained in the shadow of his floppy hood, and no sign of his hands. A stranger in a strange land. Then another younger man with a similar demeanor stepped out. Both clung to the portal frame as if it anchored them to a remnant of familiarity. Or safety. Or a firm launch platform for flight.

"WE DIDN'T DO NOTHIN'."

Smitty said, "Like we said, no problem. Can we just ask about the murder? Some bad guys invaded your neighborhood and killed somebody. They're outsiders, not from this area. One of our officers talked to two young ladies after it happened. They shared with us what they heard, which helped. If possible, we'd like to talk to them one more time. Gentlemen, we just wanna catch these creeps. I'm guessing you want that too."

"You're not all cops." Not a question, from the older hoody with a nasal accent.

"No. I'm the only cop. Zaya and Lamatte are helping me, helping us."

"So loud up here. Which one 'a you'se is the tellie?"

Smitty cocked his head. "Tellie?"

"Me. You know how it is. The cop's okay. Name's Smitty. I'm Lamatte. This is my friend, Zaya. He's investigating EMP. We just wish to talk with the girls because they might offer something else to help all of us."

"You'se guys seem okay. Wait here. Gotta ask Birdman." Mr. Nasal Voice awaited visual confirmation. Got a verbal one instead.

Lamatte said, "Sure thing. We'll wait right here. And thanks." He emphasized the words *right here* for Smitty and Zaya.

So they stood in the dark for ten minutes as gray turned into black. Every time Smitty started to speak, Lamatte shushed him.

They rocked back and forth to stay warm, but did not move. Dared not move. After the older one disappeared, the nervous one, the young one stared at them. They could not see what was in his hands under the threadbare blanket that he hugged. Nor could Lamatte sense his intentions.

Odd.

And unnerving.

19

———

"I'M BIRDMAN, FRIENDS. "WHAT'S UP?"

The three of them had waited for almost fifteen minutes in the Stygian storefront awaiting his arrival. In the reflected amber light cast by an unusual transparent globe hanging from his belt, they saw Birdman was older than his two compatriots, maybe Lamatte's age. A clean, short-cropped partial beard embraced an angular face barely visible. Smitty clipped his spot and selected *medium-dim* aimed low.

After their eyes adjusted, they saw this Birdman's deep-set eyes gleamed from under an oversized hooded sweat-shirt with a distinctive logo. It was just visible under an open floor-length topcoat. Its huge high-rise collar was framed by an integrated cape. Creased jeans, worn and scuffed but serviceable boots completed his ensemble of casual chic.

On instinct, "I'm Zaya. You ride, man?"

A look of deep skepticism transformed into vague curiosity. He said, "Used to. But my thirty-eight Flight Glide was liberated years ago. No affordable fuel around, and I'm not topside much, anyway. You? Wait. A black forty-two Commander, right?"

"Uh, yeah. That's it, brother. Not just black. Blacked out. Bars to thrusters. Full stealth. Hover low, dude."

"Hover low. Alright, again, what's up, gents?"

Smitty's slack jaw overcame gravity. He began to speak. "We'd like to—"

"How 'bout from the tellie? No offense, Officer."

"Detective."

Birdman's hooded head already began to swivel toward Lamatte with the wryest of playful grins. "What kind of name is Lamatte? Ah, Québécois. So you wanna talk with Cherry and her sister. Follow me. Don't forget to turn on your trackers. The Digs can confuse you topsiders. In case we get separated. Watch your step, gentlemen."

They couldn't see Birdman's smile, but he was sure to be enjoying himself. Smitty thought, *The Digs? Tellie? And words seem obsolete here? Jeez.*

AT FIRST, THEY TRUDGED IN SILENCE AS THEY PASSED through a portal with no door, down creaky steps, across a basement room, turning, and down more stairs, now narrower of worn stone. On at least three occasions in the first few minutes, they encountered and chose one branch of a tunnel—not another. A maze. The upper tunnel walls were constructed of curved plasticrete, then more squarish and of bricks as they descended—ancient masonry bricks, by the looks of them. More turns and more stairs, now walking on a rough stone path under close stone walls and ceilings.

After fifteen minutes at a deliberate pace, Birdman spoke as they continued their hike into the unknown. He answered specific questions not yet asked. Offered observations as they trudged on in the diffuse glow of his odd globe, augmented by Smitty's far brighter spot. That's when the sound surrounded them. They saw nothing. Feral growls echoed through the dim tunnels, from the shadows beyond their myopic beams. Squeals punctuated the louder of these. Birdman stopped and said, "Critters feed. Wild dogs don't hunt in packs in the outskirts of The Digs, but sometimes partner up with one or two others to track the bigger rats. Good eating. And the remains make decent fertilizer for the farms in the lower tunnels."

Nobody commented as they started again. Nobody was sure if he was serious. But he didn't seem the joking type.

Another fifteen minutes drifted by. They passed through smaller passages with several deviations, like a meandering dry stream. Zaya noticed alcoves along the way in which the flicker of low blue-white flames in the darkness danced in small containers. He made out hunched-over silhouettes of a figure or two in each alcove who seemed agitated by their passing. Like a natural catacomb for the still-living near the roof of Hell. Birdman now spoke in a soft and respectful voice. "Solitary souls make their homes around here. It's quiet—for those who can't emotionally tolerate the activity in our community proper, but need some proximity for support. Like a security blanket held at arm's length. Close together up here, but deeper down, these sorts spread out. Many tend the air purification fields for us. That's how they contribute."

Zaya was having the time of his life. Lamatte confided he

wanted to meet more tellies. He had learned that was their slang for telepaths—mind readers. Smitty just put one foot in front of the other wondering to what planet he was traveling, and whether he'd ever see his wife and kids again. But this Birdman elicited a certain confidence. Smitty could not explain that, nor would he try. Birdman seemed gruff but likable and articulate, like he had a million things on his mind, *and* was taking their visit seriously.

"Lots of vagrants down here. Most of us once sought low-income housing—many of us aren't employable by conventional standards—ultimately came here for a sense of community, and protection. Most birds aren't here because we're lazy. We're surviving. Most are even thriving."

At the risk of interrupting their guide's monologue, Zaya asked, "Easier to shield from EMP down here than topside?"

"Yes, that's one reason. How I got my name. How most of us found each other. There are similar communities in other places—Detroit, New York, Toronto. Much protection was already here and in other places like this. We welcome lots of immigrants from Georida, Louisitexas, Calexico, Arexico, and other places where basements and tunnels are scarce."

"*One* reason? I don't—"

"The melody is less horrible down here, not as painful, healthier harmonics. Lamatte, you get it."

Lamatte verbalized his response for Zaya and Smitty, as Birdman had. " That's one of the reasons I joined the Jesuits. Less of a cacophony. Still hurts."

NOBODY PROBED FURTHER. A DISCUSSION FOR ANOTHER TIME. Lamatte could sense profound perplexity rambling around inside Smitty and Zaya, and lots of empathy. A good thing. Birdman continued his somewhat sparse tour guide monologue as they slowly hiked, as if they were being vetted as they descended. "We have our share of nolos," and before Zaya could ask, he added, "what we call our low- or no-income folk. Poor people, either by their own choice or by someone else's topside. Like I said, some are *only* employable down here. Then we have others of means who can only thrive in communities like ours, though they may still retain interests topside. We barter a good deal. We make no apologies for our choice of lifestyle. See for yourselves."

THE TRIO STOPPED AT THE END OF A TUNNEL'S SWEEPING turn. In front of them appeared a long tunnel—straight, wide, and high—they all stared. Smitty stiffened, Lamatte sucked in a quick breath of disbelief, Zaya shook his head and glanced at the others with wide eyes. Looked more like an inviting neighborhood street than a voluminous tunnel deep under Old Chicago.

Complete with two-story pre-war *masonry* brick buildings with curtained windows, and even a few three-stories. Most glowed from within. But the *outside* space also glowed from strange globes hung on wires lining both sides of a medium-width cambered cobblestone street. They saw retail store fronts with people shopping, inside and outside. Walking the dim street seemed a surreal scene. Zaya wondered, *Who builds buildings on top of buildings, unless....* His writer's imagination already kicked into hyper-drive.

All three remained frozen in their astonishment of the sight. Birdman let them absorb the object of his pride. The Digs—Downtown. They watched dozens of people, maybe hundreds, going about their everyday lives. The relative silence jangled their ears. Folks here even walked with little sound, a lighter step. As if afraid to wake someone. As if they stood in the narthex of a large cathedral, a place of high worship.

A startling metaphysical energy was obvious in this place. Even to Smitty and Zaya. Unexplainable. These people worked and lived here because they were devout members of a homogeneous community like no other. Their humble homespun clothes, their scarcity of physical trappings... it seemed these folks transcended what so many in this world aspired to possess and display. They seemed, what? Happier for it? More contented?

Most remarkable was that which they could not see. The odor permeated everything, the odor of what? Boiled cabbage? And cinnamon? And sage? But their lungs provided a more significant clue. The air was not only heavy with odor, it was just heavy. Rich. Breathable! That's when Zaya noticed something remarkable. Nobody in sight wore a mask. Even more remarkable, nobody suffered from mask rash.

Lamatte sensed a certain reverence as he gazed down the gentle slope of this... street, this *neighborhood.* But he sensed so much more. Not much talking, no traffic noise, just a susurrus of soft footfalls and non-verbal interaction of minds embracing one another as they met their daily needs. He felt euphoric. And not just because he hadn't breathed such oxygen-rich air in a very long time. A thought came to him unbidden: *We generate our own O2, Lamatte.*

Smitty and Zaya stared down that street, then at each other. Their psychic isolation separated them from Lamatte and Birdman. Several shoppers nearby turned to stare back, but said nothing, did not point. A few subtle nods said, *Welcome.* Both men felt like they just stepped on someone else's tranquility, but found themselves forgiven for their unintentional transgression.

What happened next further escalated their sense of wonder.

20

UNDER OLD CHICAGO,
WILLIANA

THE FOUR OF THEM SAT ON A RUG, ON THE FLOOR, IN A CIRCLE, knee-to-knee. The second-story apartment faced the subterranean street less than half a mile from Lake Michigan, a million miles from *normal*. That smell again: cooked cabbage and sage. And cinnamon. They drank in the air, gulped as if they feared it wouldn't last. Their masks, now forgotten, remained clipped to carabiners on their equipment belts. None of the three topsiders said a word about it, but they shared continuous grins that spoke volumes. Smitty even playfully punched Lamatte's shoulder as they sat in silent wonder, swimming in an O2 high.

Birdman said, "Welcome to my home. I've asked someone to fetch Cherry and her sister, your witnesses. A warning, gentlemen. These girls are fragile. If I sense they feel threatened or intimidated, they're gone, and so are you."

This was not a negotiation, but terms for their ejection if they screwed up. Nobody wanted that. Too much depended on their behavior within the next few minutes in this alien environment.

THEY WERE ADORABLE. "CHERRY, STRAWBERRY, PLEASE SAY hello to my guests, Lamatte, Zaya, and Lionel."

Smitty shook his head in continued disbelief—he hadn't told Birdman his given name. Officer M'Dala from the Haley crime scene interviews did not mention these lovely girls, maybe thirteen or fourteen, were identical twins. She may not have noticed if they bundled themselves against the almost-winter chill. In sheepish school girl unison, they sang out, "Hel-lo." They widened the circle, barely room to do so. Like the adults, the twins sat cross-legged on Bird-man's faded rug, kids at a grownup gathering.

ZAYA SEEMED CHARMED AND DISTURBED. *THEY'RE SO SMALL, like porcelain dolls broken and glued back together.* He caught Birdman's gaze. His hint of a smile on the heels of his own mental simile unnerved him. A new normal, Zaya guessed.

They agreed Lamatte would lead. After reviewing what was already a matter of record, with a gentle line of questioning, Lamatte took them in a different direction. "Ladies…" The girls both beamed at that characterization. *Pre-pubescent girls are the same everywhere in some respects, even down here,* Zaya thought to himself. Another subtle smirk from Birdman. *Jeez.*

Lamatte continued. "You've told us what you heard. Now

think back to any impressions, other background noises or odors that you sensed, or any notion that crossed your minds."

Cherry scrunched her tiny nose beneath her tiny forehead nestled behind her tiny auburn bangs, eyes squeezed shut in brutal concentration, saying nothing. Her bird-like hands perched on her bony little knees. After ten seconds, her sister's eyes widened. Strawberry muttered, "Grandiose plan." Cherry opened her eyes. One remembered, the other had spoken.

With no warning, Birdman said, "Okay, thank you, ladies." The room brightened again with so many tiny almost-white teeth. "Rejoin Annie outside now, if you please. You've served well the community."

The twins popped to their feet and bounded from the room with their four pony tails and two plain skirts swinging in cadence to their skipping gait. Smitty struggled with his disappointment. Birdman said, "They had nothing else to offer, Lionel. Their aunt gave them an opportunity to experience surface noise early in their lives. That's why they were at that basement window that day. They helped as much as they were able."

Lamatte jumped in before Smitty screwed this up. "We understand, and we appreciate the opportunity to meet those lovely girls."

Birdman said, "Gentlemen, if I hadn't sensed your souls trustworthy at the surface, you would not have descended. But I am convinced you will respect this space so sacred to us."

After a soft knock, as if on cue, a petite young woman appeared through Birdman's portal. "PodGirl will escort you out. I wish you well on your quest."

Lamatte said, "Before we go, sir, you said avoiding EMP

was but one reason that brought you and many of the people here to The Digs. May I ask what else?"

"We are a simple folk who perceive more than most. We segregate ourselves to survive. For how long, we don't know. But threats more dire than EMP demand we offer cautious help when the time is right. This is one of those times."

Birdman turned to peer into Smitty's eyes. "Lionel, find your killers. You need Zaya's help." Then he turned to Lamatte. "And you must use your gift to help Zaya complete his quest. Along with you and yours." Lastly, he looked deep into Zaya's eyes. "You command a loyal audience with your podcasts, your journal. That is your strength. Some seek to silence you, do they not?" He did not await a response. "Others listen to the seeds you plant. Our planet is in jeopardy. More than you know." There was no mistaking his sincerity. He unconsciously tapped his fingers against the top of his thighs before he arose, signaling the end of the meeting.

Zaya said, "What have you not told us, Birdman?" His voice was filled with frustration.

"Evil conspires to hide the bigger truth. You already sense it but have not given it a face. EM means *Electro* and *Magnetic*. It also means *Evil* and *Money*. Ask yourselves, What is the greater truth? You might ask your guide. Seek the greater truth. Goodbye, gentlemen. Complete your quests."

SHE SEEMED A DELIGHT. THEIR GUIDE, AN EBULLIENT YOUNG lady who Birdman had introduced as PodGirl was different and charming, in a terse sort of way. Slight of build, boots for walking. Intense. Hooded like many of the others, she wore strange goggles that seemed to glow from inside the eyepieces. She talked more than Birdman, and in a less cryptic fashion. Filled with purpose, she seemed more like a topsider. Like them. Zaya asked about her moniker which sounded very un-bird-like.

"Oh, I've alienated myself from a few within the community, but Birdman keeps me close. I was once a topside energy engineer. Some stuff I know comes in handy around The Digs. Like how to communicate and broadcast up there from down here, how to generate and sustain light and heat from otherwise-inert substances, how to distill and filter air and water. I know how to generate O_2 on a sustainable basis from ground water, and how to detect the best-shielded areas. Yeah, I'm a huge anti-EMP groupie, but also a tellie. And, yes, Zaya, I think you're damn cute too."

"Oh, my. Sorry."

"Aw, don't be. The way of our world. I enjoy hanging out with islands like you. Less *head-banging,* if you know what I mean."

"Okay, so you're a caster? From down here? Me too. Up there. How come I've never heard your stuff?"

"Well, I hang out on the *Feeds Obscura.* You need an invitation. I don't get censored. Consider yourself invited, Zaya French. Can I call you PodBoy?" And just like that, Zaya knew where to find her casts.

"Really? PodBoy? You're serious? At my age? Jeez."

"You hide behind the guise of *entertainment.* Guess your reasons are valid. I present my stuff is hard-core fact, and I stand behind it. I can do that because I'm recruiting like-minders to take action more than to convince nay-sayers with entertaining stories. *And* I can hide from the bad guys here. Up there you're more exposed. I get that. By the way, did I mention I love your stories?

"Zaya, you're wondering. Yes, EMP *will* get worse, fast, from what I see on the feeds, and from what Birdman sees —which is more than most. And yes, I've got antennas and repeaters wired topside. Like you, many of us view this issue is about to explode. Think pandemic, or worse."

"Do you know about AE8897?"

"Yeah, a stepping stone to Armageddon." PodGirl then blew Zaya's sense of reality into deep space with what came next. "I forget how many words are necessary for you islands. More than I've talked in weeks. "My throat's getting sore. Let's try this. I mention a word, and you think about your reaction to that word. *Magnetosphere.* Nothing? Oh, boy. Okay, here we go." And just like that she switched to non-verbals, but she sat down to do so. This would take a lot of energy.

She planted visions of the imminent disruption of the magnetic field around the earth. Combined with other heinous crimes against nature inside the earth, these events could strip the planet of its atmosphere. Her continued thoughtstream exploded their collective sense of reality....

"Stability of the earth's core is already marginal from natural events like earthquakes and unnatural events like widespread deep drilling, fracking and attempts to seal volcanic eruptions. Together, they take their toll on the integrity of the core. Dangerous warming of the world's oceans with an obscene carbon footprint, combined with wholesale deforestation for centuries, has further unbalanced the equation. Natural events combined with man's Bigfoot print is fracturing the earth from within. And an escalating demand for natural resources far outstrips Nature's ability to replenish Herself.

"8897 is the tipping point with a high probability of trans-forming Earth into another Mars over the next few generations, or sooner. A disrupted magnetosphere combined with a disrupted

planetary core, and man will conjure the end of all life. Armageddon."

SHE PLANTED ALL THESE IMAGES—ALONG WITH A HIGH-LEVEL description of the relevant science and evidence—in their minds within a few moments and without uttering a single word. After all, verbal articulation was *so* exhausting and time-consuming. But the trio of explorers reeled from so much information of such import in so short a time.

Where Zaya had been worried of the dangers to people, he now also worried about survival of the entire planet. Lamatte reflected on Birdman's final cryptic declaration: *The greater truth eclipses the lesser truth.*

Zaya, Lamatte, and Smitty staggered from the revelation. Ever the cop, Smitty said, "If exposed, this *greater truth* would turn heads and jeopardize the passage of—" Zaya completed his sentence, "8897."

"Well, it would seem we are now loose ends too, gents, and we have our motive for the Haley case."

They had descended into these tunnels to find clues to solve a murder. They just discovered they now needed to chase the would-be murderers of Planet Earth.

LAMATTE ABSORBED THE MONUMENTAL RAMIFICATIONS OF what he'd just learned with some effort. But Zaya and Smitty faltered. They suffered headaches and nausea. Both sat down hard on a rock ledge in a musty passage halfway to the surface. Smitty vomited. Unsteady and disoriented, the men took ten full minutes to recover, breathing and sweating like marathoners nearing the finish line, before new purpose prepared them to rise and continue.

Chagrined, PodGirl said, "Sorry guys. An hour's worth of words crammed into a few seconds is harsh for you islands. But we need help, and we have little time. Besides, most of us don't wield a lot of credibility topside."

The men noticed the girl grabbed some recovery time too. It occurred to Zaya and Smitty that Birdman assigning PodGirl as their guide was a master stroke.

And Zaya sensed a deeper connection with this young woman than he'd ever experienced with anyone. What in Hell was he thinking? He had to be at least four times her age!

PodGirl just grinned.

21

S HANTAHEE,
WILLIANA
2128

TWO DECADES EARLIER, GROWING FOOD FOR TWO HUNDRED IN the dying countryside tested their faith. They made a life for themselves, but is was harsh, and sweet. They possessed purpose. The cluster of huts and surrounding fields provided their group, the faithful, sustenance—barely—an oasis in a rapidly deteriorating landscape amidst moral peril.

As a child, Fenwick Morrissee harnessed what some called amazing intuition. Likewise, his charisma served him well, and Blythe Dunning worshipped him. They were both eight years old. Fen sensed the two of them shared a natural bond. They attended many of the same Bible classes and prayer groups. They spent time together, even when forbidden, sculpting a few of their own rules under a mountain of those mandated by everyone around them. They grew up together amid this agricultural commune deep in the Shantahee Valley. They and their parents belonged to what Fen came to realize was a religious cult.

Fenwick Morrissee and Blythe Dunning married at sixteen with their parent's blessing, and with their leader's permission. Ordained at eighteen, Fen's future with Blythe also seemed pre-ordained. But Fen led a double life that troubled him, his wife and his ministry. He envisioned a different future he could no longer deny.

Something else also intruded into Blythe's thoughts, into her very being. They both knew it, but neither comprehended. During a time of creeping doubt and self-deceit, Blythe bore three beautiful children—first, a boy, and two years later, twin girls.

Fen and Blythe shared a deep bond of trust. But that bond eroded over time for no obvious reason. They both admitted this break was not a surprise to either of them at some subtle but profound level. They admitted denial of it served no useful purpose. After six years of marriage, Fen and Blythe grew estranged, so they divorced, much to the angst of their parents and their community. She moved to Toronto with their eldest child, Joshua, to be near their only family outside the commune—Fen's brother and his wife. Fen secured full custody of their two daughters and escaped to Chicago. He sensed that's where their destiny led.

Strange emotions swept Blythe into an abyss from which there was no return. So during a lucid period, Blythe surrendered custody of the four-year-old Joshua to Fen's older brother Daniel and his wife Georgia—for the child's safety. Fen supported that decision. Any alternative grew too frightening to contemplate.

Blythe's conditions of Joshua's adoption by Fen's brother

were threefold. First, they would change his name. Second, he would never learn of his biological father and mother. And third, Fen was never to contact Joshua. Daniel and Georgia accepted these terms without hesitation to make the child their own since their own tree proved barren. And Fen would honor Blythe's wishes.

Blythe passed away a year later. Fen's insight informed him she had fallen prey to the psychological impacts of a self-induced time displacement—a time cyclone—a phenomenon he wouldn't understand until much later in life. He then made a new home—a safer home—for his daughters with new friends beneath the Windy City. Away from the worsening radiation most took for granted.

A piece of Fen Morrissee died along with his childhood love, even though the heat of their passion had flickered out years earlier.

THAT WAS THEN. NOW THEY JUST CALLED HIM BIRDMAN, THE unofficial mayor of The Digs, with his twin daughters Strawberry and Cherry.

Nobody knew their birth names.

Nobody cared.

22

OLD CHICAGO, WILLIANA
2150

HE WAS *SO* TRANSPARENT. PODGIRL EXTRACTED ZAYA'S research from his mental archives during their brief time together. Then she remembered she heard much of this from one of his podcasts—he called them his *journal*—to which she subscribed. But she found picking his brain more amusing. Poor guy did not understand how much his attraction to her cute self already afflicted him.

She sat in the tiny communications alcove hollowed out of the living rock—her personal refuge deep within The Digs. Dim light emanated from two chem-globes suspended close overhead. Most of her radio and puter gear was powered down tonight. This was a time for contemplation.

If she were honest with herself, older men afflicted her.

She'd always loved Birdman, but that was different. Now this guy....

She mined a few new nuggets she hadn't heard on Zaya's podcasts. He had researched the death of someone he referred to as *an energy guy*. She found this death led to an interesting chain of events related to EMP. And *that* was *her* thing.

Zaya French was *such* an open book. Her first impression was that of a hot sticky mess gone natty. But from his well-organized and analytical mind, she extracted this:

> *"A renewable energy executive in the Washegon territory fell victim to a near-fatal accident outside Portland. A traumatic brain injury left him a vegetable. The family later pulled the plug. Cecile called when she heard that news. She informed me her father knew him."*

Fascinating. She also found the strength of Zaya's feelings for this girl, Cecile, of interest (*"I could refuse Cecile nothing. Ever"*). She wondered, *Is this going to be a problem, or is this simply the afterglow of a past infatuation? But I mustn't succumb to distractions. I need to follow this thread.*

Podgirl sent her bots to scour her extensive network of topside feeds. This energy exec—a sharp guy named Shannon Leary—specialized in efficient, high-power light-based communication media. In an obscure academic paper he wrote months before his death, he postulated this new take on wireless optical media as a desirable and practical alternative to ubiquitous dirty radio frequency communications. Light frequency *instead of* radio frequency? A fascinating premise.

Someone deleted the paper from the Journal on Communications and Energy Research, a.k.a. JOCER, and all references to it. Or so they assumed. PodGirl found a cloud copy in obscure archives on a basement server at Multnomah University, a small private institution just outside of Portland.

Brilliant, Shannon. Well-played.

From that paper, she confirmed that Leary's research *had* focused on LF, or Light Frequency communications and energy transmission to *replace* wired energy transmission and dirty RF, or Radio Frequency communication that sprayed spurious emissions like a leaky garden hose. In his paper, he said, "Think cool efficient laser instead of a hot leaky microwave." *Doesn't take a genius to see a motive to silence this smart guy if you're pimping leaky RF in AE8897.*

They silenced him before his keynote address in which he meant to surface this revolutionary technology at a prestigious energy conference. This would have impacted 8897, or at least cast serious doubt on it with a better solution. Even though LF would require up-front infrastructure investment, strategic thinkers would rally around this elegant alternative.

Shannon Leary drew a striking comparison in his paper. "RF is the coal of communication technology; LF is the wind-driven alternative. Dirty RF compared to clean LF. Whichever you choose to exploit, the science is clear."

23

CHICAGO, WILLIANA

ZAYA WASN'T A NATIVE, BUT HE LIVED IN CHICAGO FOR TWO years a while back. He knew of a nice ground-level room near O Tower, not too far from Lakeshore Drive. When away from his bus, he preferred sleeping in a room with two exits: one in front, one in back. Life in a transport, supplemented with a healthy dose of paranoia, drove his compulsion for more than one exit. These criteria limited his choices. Since street-level rooms were closest to the noise, they were cheap when available. Zaya didn't care about the noise, and he liked the low cost. Smitty's boss had promised some expense reimbursement later. Maintaining his transport and this extended investigation had strangled his savings.

Sensing... something, he stood to peer out the window. He peeked between the drawn vertical blinds that were once white. A narrow street with sparse traffic made this location ideal: cheap *and* not too noisy. Besides, the air enricher was decent.

At that moment, Zaya's implant—his skin-bud—tickled him with the subliminal message, *Voxcon Unknown Source.* Curious. Too many stories of unauthorized surveillance had always frightened him. With his current comm set, two-way voxcons still needed his manual activation via the folded device he carried in his breast pocket. Paranoia prevented him from opting for the full-auto transceiver injection a few months ago. The skin-bud was convenient for sensing important alerts from his device. Zaya had configured it to grab his attention for voxcons or textcons, but only from a VIP list he defined. Few contacts made it to this list. He manually activated full transceive by maintaining a firm pressure on his left breast pocket for two deliberate seconds. "Who is this?"

"Greetings, PodBoy. Got news."

He surprised himself at how thrilled he was by the sound of her lilting voice. It didn't take a genius to figure out how she got his number, and how she made VIP. Didn't matter.

"Hey, PGirl. Ah, did I miss a party invite or something?"

She said, "Hey, I'm thrilled by your voice too, PBoy, though yours soothes more than lilts. And I disagree—you *are* a genius."

"Aw, c'mon, girl. You can do *that thing* long distance too?"

"Well, I'm tickled to report that's only true with those who I've cemented a strong connection. Yeah, I mean you, little big man—Davey's handle for you at Joey K's Fourth Street Gym in New Wash. I don't care for that. You should tell him."

Zaya was no longer shocked when she did *that thing*— more amused, or amazed. But he wondered about impacts of the tellie population on society at large. The concepts of privacy, security, and other social, military, and political norms now needed redefinition. No words. He received her thoughts, all at once, device or no device: *"Dearest Zaya, now you know why we maintain a low profile and keep to ourselves. Besides, bombardment by countless concurrent mindstreams extracts a price. Not as if we have complete control. So I am selective in the extreme when I'm able, and use 'protection.'"* A mental wink? She reverted back to using words. "Do you feel special? Anyway, do you want my scoop on Shannon Leary, your energy guy?"

Within a nanosecond, standing alone in this seedy hotel room on a Chicago backstreet, Zaya blushed and found himself embarrassed, afraid, amused, shocked, and expectant, all at once. And more than a little weak in the knees. *How is this even possible?*

His head hurt, but his heart soared.

24

————

CHICAGO,
WILLIANA

Everyone arrived back at the captain's office in the two-five-six precinct house at 7 AM the morning after their subterranean sortie to and from The Digs, and after a short and sleepless night. Before anyone uttered a single word beyond tired salutations, Smitty made a rapid but formal ritual of maximizing the opacity of the captain's office walls. First, he faded the transparency of the three interior walls. Then he did the same to the exterior wall overlooking the Near Northside and the spires of the ancient St. John Cantius Church. He held his right arm, palm outward toward the Captain's inquisitive expression until he completed this task. Then he spoke in a solemn tone foretelling the gravitas to come.

"Captain, this will rock your world."

"Smitty, enough with the drama." She remained

standing with her hands planted on her hips, leaving no doubt she was exerting her dominance, and her rank. Smitty was well aware how much she disliked unnecessary emotionalism. But he needed to commandeer her undivided open mind before the team started lobbing mental grenades at her.

"All due respect, Cap, we *will* all sit down before proceeding. We *will* deliver our report to you as ordered. You may doubt some of this, but you *must* believe it. Now, sit. Please"

SHE LOOKED PISSED. NOT USED TO BEING ADDRESSED IN SUCH an insubordinate manner, she nevertheless followed his unusual lead. The three explorers sat across from the captain at the six-person conference table in her spacious office. From overhead and below, the auto-lighting had illuminated the now-darkened room. Captain Miners grew nervous from observing the general demeanor reflected in the three pairs of eyes that met hers with such unwavering gazes of certitude. That Smitty sat between Zaya to his right and Lamatte to his left signaled their solidarity. A cloud of dread hung heavy in the room.

As Smitty, her trustworthy down-to-earth lieutenant, related their astounding experiences of the previous afternoon, evening, and night, she sat farther back in her chair. Lamatte knew that change in body language represented astonishment more than disbelief. Her arms crossing over her chest was not a signal of cooling acceptance. She was hugging herself. She trusted evidence. And this report represented evidence from a trusted source. She impressed all three of them.

ZAYA HAD UPDATED SMITTY AND LAMATTE ON THE WAY INTO the captain's office on PodGirl's voxcon late the previous night. They now leveraged her additional insights on Shannon Leary's alleged accident and the findings of his suppressed LF research.

Zaya realized he didn't know Podgirl's real name. He'd fix that. *Are you listening, Pgirl?*

WHEN THEY FELL SILENT, CAPTAIN MINERS KNEW THEY MUST follow the evidence to move forward. With the entire unedited story in the open, she began, ignoring the larger magnetosphere issue for the moment.

She said, "Okay. Wow. A lot to absorb. Um, I need to breathe!" After a couple of noisy deep breaths, the captain rubbed her sweaty palms together in front of her on the table. "First, you gained another piece of intel when that little girl said she heard, 'Grandiose plan.' Let's start there. What do we do with that? What does it mean?"

Lamatte said, "I sensed the slightest pause as Strawberry articulated that phrase, as if she heard three words, not two. 'Grandi Ose Plan?'"

As they all processed what that might mean, ever the researcher, Zaya's thumbs and index fingers pummeled his device, now unfolded on the table in front of him. "Hey, guys, guess what my favorite search engine just popped? Care to guess the name of Grandy Group's Chief Financial Officer? Carmen Rios. What if they heard 'Grand Rios Plan', or 'Grandy's Rios Plan?'"

She had shuddered, blinked a few times and said, "Holy shit!" Smitty *never* heard Cap swear.

He said, "Is it possible Rios from Grandy contracted with the Capitol Security Service— SS—to whack Secretary Haley? And then covered up this whole magnetosphere thing until Libby Blade's bill became policy?"

Captain Miners still reeled from revelations of the last twenty minutes. But ever the cop, she started counting off relevant suppositions. "First, motive: the proconsul's ambition to pass that damn telecom bill and to squash any opposition to its passage. Second, means: Security Service thugs, assuming they do wet work, could get this done. Third, opportunity: the Secretary's trip off-calendar and off-campus to visit our fair city. Fourth, timeline: the urgency to pass this bill before the media gets their hooks into this LF or magnetosphere news. And fifth, ear-witness testimony: the young birds' statements that '*she* oughta be pleased'—*she*. Libby Blade?—and 'Rudest job for *SS* yet?'—*SS*. As in the Capitol Security Service?

"Zaya, your theory says that another four murders besides Haley's are part of a related cover-up. Assuming its validity, this constitutes a conspiracy from a policy enforcement perspective, or even treason against the United Westicas, contingent on more substantive evidence." The captain rubbed her neck as she continued. "But we're basing much of this on anecdotes and hearsay from a little girl and a psychic who live in the sewers of Old Chicago. Neither are in custody, nor are they willing to testify in court, not that a court trial would ever happen. Or if it did, their credibility would be questionable."

"Tunnels, not sewers, Cap."

Captain Miners punished Smitty with a withering look of annoyance. She was firing for effect, anyway. Her gears ground as she shifted into hyper-drive. "Whatever. Our working theory implies an influential member of the UWT Assembly of Elders orchestrated a major conspiracy and a half-dozen murders."

"Five murders." Zaya bit his lower lip, hard, as soon as he spoke.

"Again! Whatever! A conspiracy that affects the entire planet, maybe even its very survival? Je-ZEUS! We need a helluva lot more before this working theory leaves this team. Are we as one?"

In chorus: "Yes, sir."

"And all this other 'sensing' stuff? Soft. Not sure I can even get behind all that."

Lamatte, reluctant to speak after the captain had snapped at Smitty and Zaya, did so anyway. There was just too much at stake. "Captain, everything about Secretary Haley's case starts and stops with you, at least until they take it away. You're an outstanding leader. You will follow the evidence, and you trust your people. Or we wouldn't even be here. You're conflicted between the monumental ramifications of these discoveries, your personal credibility, and protecting the daughter nobody knows you brought into this world thirteen years ago. Same age as Cherry and Strawberry. You gave her up for adoption to a wonderful family in Minneapolis, Captain. That speaks to your wish for her absolute well-being. Now you've surrendered any possibility of bearing another child. As a practical matter—and with an aggressive career that has consumed your life—you'll do anything to make sure your beautiful daughter has a planet to grow up on." Lamatte realized he'd said far too much. Lowered his head.

She muttered under her breath with a tone of abject surrender. "Son-of-a-bitch."

Smitty said, "Fucks with your mind, don't it, Cap?"

She clenched shut her eyes as if absorbing a brutal blow to the gut. She opened her eyes to look into his. "Who *are* you, Lamatte? Then *the captain* reappeared. "Okay, let's say I'm there. But if any of you breathe one freaking word of what Mr. Insensitive here just said, I will hurt you." And she smiled.

They needed help. Big help they could trust.

25

———

CHICAGO,
WILLIANA

CED Captain Judge Miners sat alone in her office at the two-five-six contemplating the voxcon she was about to initiate. This call would place a series of events in motion that once started could not be stopped. She had occupied this office for almost two years, but she now saw it in a different light. Between the glossy black conference table at which she sat, surrounded by six shiny black chairs, a flat-white ceiling and lighted floor, the dramatic contrast of this space struck her. *Could the anatomy of my impromptu investigatory team be more high-contrast than this silly office? A stalwart detective, a journalist who broadcasts entertaining stories that <u>might</u> be fact, and a damn psychic!*

Then she smiled. They were getting results when no one else could. She shook her head back just enough to adjust her damn bangs, once again tempted to just hack them off.

Bangs were easy and practical, but could be distracting. Occurred to her she needed a trim, especially the back of her shaven neck. Captain Miners took a deep breath and stood up for the voxcon that would likely jeopardize her stellar career. Standing at attention seemed the right thing to do when egregiously breaking protocol.

"ALLIANCE INTELLIGENCE AGENCY, CHICAGO FIELD OFFICE. How may I direct your call?"

"This is Captain Judge Miners of the Chicago Enforcement Department, badge number 405-580. I need to speak with your Executive Special Agent in Charge—right now. This is an urgent matter of Alliance security."

"Yes, ma'am. Re-directing your call. Please hold."

Captain Miners wasn't sure why the 'please hold' irritated her, just a little. Ten seconds later—

"This is ESAIC Blake, Captain. You mentioned a matter of Alliance security? How may I help?"

Blake pronounced ESAIC as 'E-sake' as if everyone should know what that rarified and pretentious title meant. But he seemed nice enough. Captain Miners said, "ESAIC Blake, you can help by listening with an open mind. This is not *just* a matter of Alliance security. I am violating chain-of-command protocol here due to this matter's urgency. It concerns my case—SecDef Madeleine Haley's homicide— but that's only the beginning. Meet with me and my team this morning, or regret it."

"Ten o'clock, Captain, my office. One Alliance Plaza, one hundred-eightieth floor."

Click.

Wow!

· · ·

THIS REQUIRED A GROUP EFFORT. BECAUSE OF THE SOFT nature of the team's investigatory methods, Captain Miners brought her trio of intrepid explorers with her to see ESAIC Edmond Blake of the prestigious AIA. An assistant awaited their arrival at the elevator and ushered the quartet in to see her boss. Overlooking the three-story museum and twenty-story memorial spire on the site of the Sears Tower far below, Blake's austere office also commanded a magnificent view of the lake and of the city center's muted skyline. But its tiny interior surprised her the most. The conference table dominated the room and doubled as Blake's desk. One executive desk chair and five commodious guest chairs were all the room's diminutive dimensions allowed. Not even a puter.

After introductions and handshakes, but almost no small talk, Captain Miners captured Lamatte Foliére's gaze. He rewarded her with a subtle nod that said, *We can trust this guy. Do not lie or embellish.* Not that she would. The Captain took a moment to reflect how her interviewing, interrogation, and investigative methods had evolved in the last three hours. The Captain briefed AIA executive with occasional corrections and color added by her team. She no longer bristled when they did so. ESAIC Blake wore an iron mask of neutrality.

The group agreed to postulate much of their story based on Zaya's private investigation over the course of the last year. They would minimize the involvement or specifics related to The Digs. At first, Captain Miners resisted this notion, but capitulated because of the unique nature of their sources. With that constraint, Captain Miners threw the full weight of her office behind the results of Zaya's investigation as she understood them, as well as the shocking postulations they learned underground.

Blake seemed frozen in his chair. Torso canted right, his

right elbow rested on the table. With his chin and ever-so-slight jowls nested on the three knuckles and thumb of his right hand, his extraordinary jaw jutted forward. A curved index finger tucked just above and to the right edge of his stern lips. Fifteen minutes later, expecting accusations of weak policy work and over-active imaginations, Blake surprised them yet again. His iron facade cracked as he smiled. An ebullient voice came to life along with a million-lumens grin. He said, "Well done, Captain and team. I am impressed at how much you've deduced with so little hard evidence. I won't ask how you achieved that. You've provided additional useful intel for our investigation into this Libby Blade affair, as well as corroboration of elements we only suspected. Thank you. Now in brief, I can share this with you.

"Several arrests are imminent through a coordinated series of coast-to-coast and tundra-to-cape indictments for serial murder, conspiracy, and treason. These arrests include members of the Assembly of Elders, the Capitol Security Service, and the Grandy Group, not to mention a small cadre of their remote operatives. That's the long and short of it. I apologize I am not at liberty to divulge more at this moment, and I must now swear you to secrecy under penalty of law." He waited with solemnity for each to nod their oath.

"Captain, at the appropriate time I will inform your commander that you and Detective Smith handled this case with extraordinary finesse on behalf of the CED. We're projecting these apprehensions to happen within days. And I will explain that circumstances mandated your protocol breech."

The Captain and Smitty offered a professional smile of gratitude and another nod.

"Mr. French, I must warn you—no podcast, journal or publication of any kind until we authorize it. I will commit to personally letting you know the moment you are free to broadcast. You will have first shot at this complete story going public. Whether you do so under the guise of entertainment is up to you. Fair? And Zaya, I am a big fan of *The Alley* when I find the time." He grinned and winked.

"Yes, sir! And thank you." Zaya goofy-grinned back. Not professional. He didn't care.

Still facing Zaya and locked onto his eyes, ESAIC Blake said, "Mr. Foliére, I'd be glad to exchange thoughts with you anytime." He then sideways glanced at Lamatte across the table and winked. Again. Nobody except Lamatte took notice beyond what appeared to be a simple departure remark.

Everyone's heads swam.

THEY RODE IN SILENCE DURING THEIR HALF-MINUTE DESCENT from the one-hundred-eightieth floor to where their lev transport awaited in its ninth floor parking bay. Captain Miners had suggested they reserve comments for a de-brief in her office. With Smitty at their transport's stick, their silence continued during the entire four-minute flight to the two-five-six.

LAMATTE WAS BURSTING TO SPEAK, BUT WAITED. ONCE SEATED again at the Captain's conference table with the windows opaqued, he blurted, "Blake is a tellie! He knew our entire story seconds after we entered his office!"

Just when this team imagined their scenario couldn't grow much more bizarre, it had. After a few moments of absorbing yet another epiphany, the Captain smiled a toothy grin. Her fears of lost credibility evaporated. Her world had already changed forever. But of greatest import, it was enough to know they would help stop ruthless greed-mongers from destroying Monica's future. Her little girl would meet boys, get into trouble, maybe marry, make babies, and live happily ever after. Well, that might be a stretch, but she indulged herself in that fantasy for a few moments knowing this team contributed to saving the world. Or at least delaying its destruction. *And* her long-standing high-profile murder case was about to close, at last. She needed to brief her commander per ESAIC Blake's instructions. She'd take a temporary hit for the end-run, but Blake assured he'd fix that soon. Good enough.

26

New wash, Maryginia

Could this be true? Proconsul Libby Blade worried she was in too deep. She imagined her opulent office in the Longworth Assembly office building had become a prison cell. Opponents to her signature legislation, 8897, were spewing a cinematic-caliber drama called magnetosphere disruption, a connection only made in private—so far. *And* that such a phenomenon could cause temporary or permanent damage to the entire planet. If this were true, she would be the rich magister on a dead planet. How did she let matters get this far? Her favorite search engine dredged up some scary facts about this magnetosphere thing:

- Envelopes our planet and protects us from the fury of the Sun,

- Absorbs the incoming energy from the solar wind and releases that explosive energy in the form of geomagnetic storms and sub-storms,
- Without the magnetosphere, powerful solar particles could strip the Earth of its protective layers,
- After Mars lost the protection of its magnetosphere, solar wind stripped away most of its atmosphere, leaving it a barren planet devoid of all life.

HOW HAD SHE LET MATTERS GET THIS FAR? SHE HAD ORDERED atrocities. That was troubling enough. They were necessary to silence those who jeopardized her strategy. One did what one must for the greater good. If it were only about re-tasking satellites from some snowflake climate mission to enable better communications and faster Internet for her constituents and for all her future voters? *That* is what got her behind 8897 with all of her formidable resources.

But if she shouldn't worry about this magnetosphere crap, like she was being told, why had NASA watched its condition with such intensity for the last one-hundred-thirty-five years? They even continued that mission after privatizing NASA when every dime mattered—the Magnetospheric Multi-scale Mission, or MMS. She just had to wonder. And doubt.

Libby initiated a voxcon with the Grandy Group's CFO. She needed assurances. "Carmen, can this be true? If there's even a chance—"

"Settle down, Madame Proconsul. The flakes always come up with reasons to stop or slow progress."

Not to be so easily mollified, she pressed on, "And then there's the other issue. If we don't get 8897 passed before this LF stuff catches on, we'll lose critical support. That loss will also jeopardize our success."

His smooth tone inspired trust. "That energy guy made some noise. Now there is silence. Besides, the RF technology is ready to deploy, but that LF stuff would take years of research and a helluva lot more investment in infrastructure. Look how long fiber optics took back in the day. So let's get this done, Libby, and we won't need to worry. By the time 8897 gets passed, it'll be too late."

They concluded their voxcon.

Her second assistant announced, "Madame Proconsul, you have a caller. A rough young lady is here to see you."

"Is she on the calendar?"

"Ma'am, do you have a daughter?"

Libby's heart leaped into her throat. Her face reddened. "Send in the young lady, please. Clear my calendar for the next hour."

"But—"

"Joss!"

"Yes, ma'am."

Sierra Blade, a.k.a. PodGirl, was desperate enough to visit her estranged mother, Elizabeth Blade, ProConsul of the Assembly of Elders for the United Westican Territories. She had contemplated this moment the entire seventeen-minute hyper-lev flight from Chicago to New Wash. She *hated* exposure outside The Digs, much less, traveling to see her mother.

This was so hard! But the life of her planet might very well be at stake. Sierra stopped just inside her mother's office portal after closing the door behind her, hands folded with respect in front of her. Winded, she said, "Mother."

With a formal voice steeped in proper diction, Proconsul Blade said, "Sierra. What brings you by?"

"Not much changes, does it? We haven't seen each other in four years."

"Sorry. Lots of stress. Not much time, so—"

"You are correct. Not much time. For any of us. One word, Mother. Magnetosphere. Reaction?" Nobody spoke for thirty seconds.

"Sierra, if you need money—"

"No, Mother, what I need is for you to prevent Armageddon. Grant me and everyone life. Kill 8897. Before it's too late."

"Oh, Sierra, that conspiracy nonsense again?"

"Mother, I know what you believe, and I've seen evidence of what you've done to support your beliefs."

"You know nothing."

"Nothing? Well, let's review, shall we?" Proud of her eidetic memory, Sierra enjoyed reciting complex lists. She ticked her points off on her fingers. "2148, January: climatologist's *suicide* in Ithaca, New York; February: energy exec's *accident* outside Portland; March: Grandy policy exec's *suicide* in Palo Alto; May: your own aide's lethal *overdose* in Georgetown; Ongoing: *blackmail* of a local priest, for God's sake, who you had finger your own aide for death by one of your thugs named Dean, or one of *his* thugs. One of your own aides had correlated these activities to ram 8897 into policy and *overdosed*. Then in June of the same year, your most vocal opponent of 8897, Secretary of Defense Haley, *murdered* in Chicago.

"They all stood to impede the passage of your precious bill, Mother, and now they are *all dead*. All coincidences? All for a bill that will strip our planet of its protection from solar radiation? A bill that could very well fuel Earth's next and final extinction event? Was that your aim all along, Mother? If not, this needs to stop. Now. Or there *will* be no stopping it. For any of us."

"Sierra, I don't expect you to understand the concept of the greater good, so I won't try. How can you know all this?" But Madame Proconsul could guess, couldn't she?

"My God, Mother, you're not listening! Start practicing a new mantra, *'Death to all life, but our intentions were for the greater good.'* The end! But for now, forget about what *will* happen. Do you want to see what's happening *right now?* Those of us who have long feared EM poisoning have studied it more than anyone still alive. The accredited scientific community is now supporting everything we've been saying for years. And EMP is but one symptom your bill will proliferate. I don't live underground just because I am some crazy conspiracy nut. I brought evidence."

SIERRA APPROACHED THE PROCONSUL STANDING NEAR HER desk at a deliberate pace, prepared to back away again. She reached into the cloth bag hanging on her left hip with its shoulder strap diagonal across her chest. She pulled out a small but heavy device. Depressed what was obviously a power tab. A soft hum tickled the senses. Barely perceptible.

Lots of gold and copper-colored alloys, and a heavy fabric strap with shiny threads woven into it. The eyepieces shimmered with a subtle iridescent glow.

"These goggles are a tactical item that allows the human eye to see EM beams. Right now. These are currently calibrated to only show beams a thousand times stronger than are safe for our physiology. It's even worse for animal and plant life. Each beam through your skull is equivalent to sticking your head in a microwave and hitting *cook* for two seconds. And the effect is cumulative. This is happening *this instant* regardless of what your politician's mind tells you. With 8897, your satellite cloud will *rain* this poison down on us from space, and with far more damaging power. Think *radiation poisoning.* And bouncing those beams from tower to ubiquitous tower, that two-second cook time increases to ten seconds or more. Each. Virtually non-stop. Use your imagination. Here. Satisfy your curiosity. You are a brilliant woman, and you will understand. Seeing is believing. Look —right now—in this room. Go ahead, Mother."

With some reticence, Libby took the goggles from Sierra. She held them against her face with both perfectly manicured hands. She was looking at her daughter through the goggles' lenses when she did so. As she watched, a near-horizontal green beam in sharp relief to the surrounding room pierced and passed through Sierra's head like an arrow from left to right with no prelude. Then it was gone. Another beam stabbed her daughter through the chest before disappearing just as quickly. Libby jerked the goggles away from her face as if she suspected a nasty parlor trick. Then she returned them to her face and swiveled in place. She could not look away. A beam struck down from overhead, through the ceiling, and passed between them like a soundless bolt of near-vertical green lightning. Just as fast, she noticed dozens of beams comprising various hues of green darting all around them at random angles. She shuddered, handed the device back to Sierra as if they were hot, or as if the sight disgusted her.

Sierra accepted the goggles and forged ahead, realizing she was playing a most dangerous game. "The latest generation of telecommunication technology subjects us to microwave rays. That's their frequency. No one argues this point, Mother. Strong microwaves cook food. The only thing that stops them from cooking the cooks is a built-in metal shield. Take away that shield and the cook gets cooked. This 10G technology is bombarding us with beams between countless towers and between millions of networks and billions of personal and business devices. With the cloud of satellites enabled by your bill, Mother, these separate beams turn into non-stop *clouds of poisonous radiation*. No place will be safe. We'll bake our brains and our bodies with lethal radiation. Ongoing. And as the even more potent 11G tech emerges, imagine the resulting *pandemic*. Worse, much worse than even such a lethal pandemic of illness and death, the earth's magnetosphere could stop working. It already interacts differently with damage we've done to the earth's magnetic core over the centuries."

Sierra's mother stood by her desk, a statue incapable of conjuring any response to what could only sound like a compelling case for catastrophe.

Sierra continued, "This will have the *irrevocable* effect of disrupting our planet's entire magnetosphere. At that point, we will no longer need to worry about EMP. Because we won't have air to breathe and the sun will broil everything on earth, including you and me. And fast. End of Earth. We become another Mars."

"Sierra, you're dredging up that tired old argument? Do you have proof?"

"The proof will be a scorched planet—and your proof will arrive too late. But the science is compelling right now. Even if you doubt the truth of this science, is it worth the risk? Jeez, Mother, for all our sakes, stop this insane bill from becoming policy. At least re-examine the science before it does! Why would I make this up? What do I have to gain? Mother... Mom, with your finesse, you can make this work, can't you? So you take a hit for killing a bill you've been advocating. But with new scientific information now at your disposal, you could go down in the history books as the savior of our wounded planet!"

"Sierra, you realize how crazy all this sounds, right?"

"Okay, if you can't wrap your mind around the big-picture because of personal beliefs, or self-interest, or whatever, let's simplify the discussion. How do you feel about high treason?" As she fell silent to let that question sink in, Sierra held up a small leather-bound journal that Libby recognized in an instant.

"*Lucy's journal?* She went nowhere without that. How—"

In a lower voice Sierra interrupted. "Tess? Temp?"

As she uttered these two words and waited, Sierra observed Libby's reaction. With surprise, Sierra was met with a blank expression. A complete lack of comprehension. She decided the time may have arrived for something she feared above all else—probing her estranged mother's mind. Rivers of sweat ran from Sierra's armpits inside her home-woven sweatshirt with its thick cowled hood thrown back onto her vest that reflected a metal sheen. Her forehead glistened, matting the brown hair onto her forehead. *Can I only probe her thoughts relevant to this discussion?* She doubted that. But she must know!

"What is it you think you know, Sierra? Why do you suggest I'm committing treason? Whatever else you think, I am no traitor."

"You don't know, do you?" As Sierra explained TESS and TEMP to her mother—the scheme to assassinate people from space without government sanctions—Libby shuddered. Her certitude faltered. Sierra could hear it. Even without probing her thoughts.

"Um, if what you say is true, which I find difficult to believe, this would indeed constitute treason. I, well, we must look into this further. May I have that journal?"

"You may not, Mother, but if you're inclined to tip the scales of justice toward righteous indignation, I suggest you do so with dispatch. Here is a copy of the relevant passages." She handed over a micropod. "I will return Lucy's original journal to someone I trust, at least until I can trust you further, Mother. Responsible parties already hold complete copies. As you well know, secrets cannot remain secret for long in New Wash. Or so I'm told. I am giving you the chance to get ahead of this. I suggest you use this intel to your advantage. Help us save the earth. Help yourself by defeating traitors from within what's left of your beloved democracy. If you find you can trust the truth of *this*, maybe you'll believe the rest of it. My sources are unimpeachable. Are yours? If for no other reason, act fast for your own self-preservation. I'm no politician, Mother, but it would appear your handlers are handling you. What will you do now?"

Libby told her strange but well-informed daughter she would perform due diligence with sources other than her traditional network. That's all she could commit.

"That's good enough for me. For now."

"Can I borrow those goggles?"

"Keep them. Use them. I have another pair to get me home." She thrust the goggles toward her mother who snatched them eagerly and held them close.

"How do I reach you, Sierra?"

"You don't. I will reach you, Mother. I promise." Sierra paused, looked her mother in the eye for a long beat, and spoke in a soft but solemn tone. "Mother, Madame Proconsul, I ask little of you, other than my privacy. But I *beg* you to exercise haste and diligence in this matter. Or we'll all suffer the most dire circumstances. And Mother?"

"Yes... Daughter?" It was as if Libby just conceded some emotional point by uttering that familiar but difficult word.

"Be very careful. You are now a loose end, too." With that, Sierra left the headlight goggles clutched to her mother's breast. She tucked the small battered journal back into her shoulder bag, flipped up her heavy hood after planting a second pair of goggles around her neck, and wheeled on her heel. She opened the office portal and left at a quick pace.

---

ierra hated busy sidewalks. They were too noisy, too exposed, and too unpredictable. She struggled just to walk among the throng. That did not distract her from sensing immediate danger among the mental muddle. She passed a transport at the curb to her left in a near-silent low hover with its curbside portal open to a darkened interior. She did not see the needle approaching the back of her neck, but she sensed it. Someone—a scarred hulk of a man —was about to stab her through the fabric of her hood! She listened to this man's mind mulling over every word that had just passed between Sierra and her mother. How? She couldn't understand what this thug heard, only that he heard it all. His thoughts rattled around in some foreign language. *No time for that, not now!* Sierra dropped face down onto the filthy sidewalk, away from the needle, amidst hundreds of other pedestrians too busy to notice one strange girl wearing goggles under a hoodie. She screamed and rolled onto her back, staring up into his eyes.

Startled, her attacker still held the syringe in one hand, reached down to clutch a handful of her loose clothing with his other. His intent was clear. He meant to subdue and kill Sierra, throw her into the transport. Before he could grab her, she rolled under that transport, felt the tingle of its hover field, and came out the far side, into traffic. She stayed low. Standing up now meant certain injury or death. No vehicles contacted the smooth but grimy surface between her and the far curb. As a steady stream of vehicles—likely most or all on auto-drive—passed inches above her at speed, she rolled and kept rolling until she reached the far side of this busy side street off Independence Avenue. *God, I hate this city. Now I have one more reason.* Once she reached the far curb, she crawled up onto the sidewalk, stood, and dusted herself off before disappearing into the throng.

Did my mother just try to abduct or kill me? Or was it her handlers? More likely, the latter. Does she know they've bugged her office? The ruffian's intent was clear. She thought, *Not to this girl. Not today.*

"MOTHER!"

"Sierra, what—"

"Do not say another word. Your office is bugged. Someone is surveilling you. Whoever that is just tried to kill me in the street right outside your building. They heard every word we said. Mother, you're endanger. Get out, *right now! TRUST NO ONE!*"

Libby's heart thundered in its attempt to escape her chest. She saw bright spots as the blood pounded in her temples. Sierra had no reason to fabricate such a story. Grabbing a wrap and her shoulder bag after inexplicably tossing Sierra's goggles into it, she rushed out of her office, past Andrea's and Joss's desks in the outer reception area.

Left wordlessly with her cape billowing in her wake. She heard the vague plea from Andrea asking her intent, but ignored everything except calculating the quickest way out. She'd take the stairs down four flights. Nobody ever used the stairs. Tapped her temple. "Clark, limo, alley, right now. No security detail. Bring your kit."

"Yes, ma'am,"

28

NEW WASH, MARYGINIA

PROCONSUL BLADE HAD NO WORDS. SHE SAT IN SHOCK IN THE rear of her limo with Clark at the wheel. She raised the partition between them. Libby Blade, one of the most powerful and influential women of her generation, felt like a helpless little girl.

Long shadows drifted by as they floated through a hazy evening twilight. The only physical reminder of her estranged daughter's bizarre visit now lay in her lap. And the doubt. The scenario her daughter's visit painted in her mind was no longer the worst nightmare she might conjure. The unusual pair of goggles festooned with dull gold, silver and brown gadgets were a reminder of what might be far worse. Everything of which she felt so confident became a wavy mirage in the last thirty minutes. Who was watching and listening, and why? She knew why. Was this limo bugged too?

She rummaged through her doubts over this magnetosphere discussion with Carmen Rios. But he had so easily dispelled her uneasiness with words of confidence. Shit! He *was* handling her. But she had ignored it because he was financing the bulk of her bid for magister! It warranted a bid for nothing if.... *Oh my God!*

Savvy politicians sense when to cut and run, and Libby was a savvy politician. Her bid for the Oval Office had just evaporated under suspicion of treasonous acts, including her own unwitting role. Someone had just attacked her daughter. Was she next? Now she'd be happy just to survive the night.

Someone would pay!

Libby entertained no delusions of innocence. Even with plausible deniability for accidental deaths and suicides, she shared in the guilt in generous measure. She'd have to live with that. But despite all the maneuvering, Libby still viewed herself a patriot. There just was no *greater good* in Grandy's TESS/TEMP strategy. Not that she really understood *Targeted Exposure from Surveillance Satellites* or *Targeted ElectroMagnetic Poisoning*. But neither sounded legal *nor* patriotic.

Sierra was right—she now dared trust no one. How would she proceed? Anyone could track searches easier than voxcons. Countless watchers tracked her calendar as well as her comings and goings. Was she being followed even now? She'd have to take a chance. If she too was now a loose end in tying up a conspiracy, she saw much more at stake than political goals or catching traitors. That said, Libby needed confident provenance before risking her entire life's work.

Libby initiated a whispered voxcon on her implant. The deep voice said, "Agent Harley Blade."

"Hello, Father. I need a favor."

"Libby-girl!"

"Can I come to your apartment for a visit?"

"Love it! Later today? I'm home around eight-ish."

DESPERATE TIMES. AFTER CLARK DROVE HER AROUND FOR two hours to make sure nobody followed them—Clark possessed anti-surveillance skills as an erstwhile Secret Service agent—she arrived at her father's thirty-second-floor studio condo near downtown New Wash. Not much of a view. A small balcony faced southwest and other buildings close by as seen through the perennial haze. Too hot in the evenings, so the blinds stayed closed all the time, anyway.

Supervisory Special Agent Blade's Spartan furnishings were at least twenty years old. He seldom stayed in his apartment except to sleep. Some nights. Ate all his meals out. Libby shook his hand as she entered. He knew better than to offer a hug.

"Father, I apologize for being direct, but I'm short on time. I couldn't risk a voxcon. Who is your most trusted friend at AIA?"

"Ah. Oh, that's easy. My old partner, Eddy Blake. Last I heard, he was running the Chicago field office. He's on that high-profile Haley murder. Feds have been working with the locals."

"Would you trust him with your life?"

"Already have. And vice versa. Got ugly more than once together in the field. Now we're both too old, which is bullshit. But neither of us forgets. A mutual debt. What's going on, Libby-girl?"

"Better you don't know."

Harley cast his head and eyes downward before raising just his eyes to peer into his daughter's. Shook his head. She was already placing his safety in jeopardy just by being here. In a worried voice, the hardened AIA agent said to his distant daughter, "Ah, yes. You politicians are huge on plausible deniability. That's because none of you knows how to keep a secret. Want an introduction?"

She wondered if this Blake could keep his mouth shut. "Thanks. I owe you. Tomorrow?"

"Yes, you do owe me. And yes, tomorrow, *if* I can reach him. You're a VIP. He'll talk with you."

"How's Mother?"

"Ask *her*. We don't talk since the divorce. She lives in the middle of nowhere back in Montanaho. Always eccentric. I never understood her. A lot like my granddaughter, I imagine. How is little Sierra?"

"Thank you, Father. I need to run. If he'll meet with me, it needs to be outside official New Wash. Ask him to call my personal cell with when and where in Chicago after tomorrow noon, so I can catch lunch with my father's old friend and partner."

Agent Blade seemed suddenly distracted. He held up an index finger after tapping his temple. "Agent Blade—"

Libby offered a small wave, turned to leave.

"What? Thank you." A quick tap disconnected the voxcon. "Libby, wait. It seems someone just blew up your office. Your staff was killed instantly."

Not sure she heard him correctly, her eyes became saucers of disbelief just before her knees buckled. Harley helped her toward a kitchen chair, but she recovered and pulled away. She had already jeopardized his safety just by being here. Within seconds, she recovered, donning a dangerous demeanor that visibly frightened her father.

"Father, I must go."

"Libby-girl, protocol says I should take you into protective custody."

"No offense, Father, but fuck protocol. I've got this."

He knew better than to object. Besides, she swept from the apartment before he dared reach out to her again.

29

———

C HICAGO,
   WILLIANA

———

Detective Lionel Smith—Smitty—said the captain was busting his chops about catching up on reports. "Credibility, Smitty! No fiction or fantasy. Figure out how to document our case with the *evidence* at hand." Smitty scratched his head, slumped over his desk. He dictated a few words, and then spent more time muttering, "delete last three sentences, start a new freakin' paragraph."

———

Meanwhile, Lamatte and Zaya hunkered down in the two-five-six's near-deserted break room. Lots of activity outside, but in here, only the soft hum and whispered movement of the auto-server. At last, both retreated to introspection once the server set a steaming bio-foam mug of rocket fuel in front of each of them. Zaya reacted to Lamatte's glum demeanor. "*What*, already? We should be basking in the recognition of our work. Serious progress on the Haley case, one step closer to saving the planet. The usual stuff. Spill!"

With a gaze downcast under heavy lids, Lamatte mumbled as he puttered with the rancid cup of go-juice in front of him. He slumped. "Zaya, I can't count the reasons Maria is so special to me. She reads people, including me, better than I. We understand each other. We empathize, and that makes us blind to so much else. It's as if our minds close a curtain to protect us from our own vulnerabilities."

"And your vows?"

"Not sure you understand this, Zaya, but you are my only friend. I have no one else. Sorry to burden you with this."

"You kidding? I'm honored. The truth? I don't have friends either. Except for you. And Smitty. I don't pretend to understand this whole telepathy or empathy thing, but I can tell you this. Doesn't take a psychic, or whatever, to see that you and Maria belong together. Seems like we saw quite a few contented folks in The Digs. Look, Lamatte, relationships are tough no matter who you are. I've been a loner my entire long life. Three times I've intersected with a kindred spirit, for lack of a better term. Those times gave a special meaning to my life. Their passing left me hollow and doubting myself for not prioritizing them. Are you willing to fight for her?"

"Zaya, I'm afraid."

"Tough shit, soldier, chew harder. We'll figure this out. Together. Catch the bad guys, make them hurt, protect Maria, live happily ever after. Deal?"

"I love how you do that, my friend. Yes, it's a deal. I must confess, I sensed more comfort in those tunnels than anywhere I've traveled. Would you think me crazy if I wanted to return? Maybe with Maria? For a while, at least?"

"Hey, man, Crazy is a relative term, dude."

30

Anderson Dean was pleased with himself. He had finally aligned with the right players at the right time. But then the proconsul's daughter came out of nowhere with intel that could ruin everything. Retif screwed up by failing to grab her. And he had really looked forward to tucking a magister in his pocket. Oh, well. That's politics. The ambitious bitch had to go. But they found only two bodies. Neither was Libby's. Somehow, despite her predictability, she'd disappeared. Maybe she had a little game after all.

Agent Dean, Proconsul Blade is asking for you. Will you take the call?"

"Yes, thank you."

"Hello, Anderson. Did you plant that little surprise in my office, or was it that monster you keep on such a short leash?"

"Madame Proconsul, Libby, I'm so happy you're okay. I didn't—"

"Cut the bullshit, Dean, you tried to kill me, you son-of-a-bitch. Worse, you attacked my daughter. Now I've killed you."

"What—"

Whump!

31

C HICAGO,
WILLIANA

YET ANOTHER DEFINING MOMENT. IT OCCURRED TO LIBBY THIS was the first time she'd traveled anywhere alone in a very long time. *And I have never felt so alone.* The twenty-two-minute private limo flight ended at the one-hundred-eightieth floor VIP parking bay of One Alliance Plaza. She walked alone to the Midwestern Headquarters of the Alliance Intelligence Agency. She didn't know how she would approach Executive Special Agent in Charge Eddy Blake, her father's ex-partner and trusted friend.

It seemed Blake had been expecting her call. Or her office impressed him, because he offered to clear his calendar for this meeting. Libby traveled incognito. Her elaborate fashion mask featured ornate twin tricklers with a state-of-the-art air-gel cushion around its perimeter to prevent the rash so common from the cheap masks worn by the pedestrian masses.

Though that impossible-to-acquire mask became superfluous the moment she entered the air-enriched limo in the New Wash VIP commuter port, it remained in place. Nor was it necessary upon exiting the transport. Still, she wore that mask. Nobody noticed. The building's perimeter curtain insulated them from what was called *street air*. She knew all Alliance buildings maintained an oxygen-rich atmosphere.

Blake personally greeted her as she stepped into the expansive executive suite of AIA Chicago. Agent Blake wore a few extra pounds with dignity. He was handsome, courteous and imposing. His impeccable appearance impressed her. Libby liked him already—she admired men who paid close attention to their appearance.

Once ensconced in ESAIC Blake's office with the walls opaqued, only then did Libby shed her disguise. Off came the mask, the floppy hat, and the mirrored solar shields. After she took the proffered seat at his combo desk and conference table, she fluffed and smoothed her straight and short strawberry-blonde hair—this week's color. She felt small in that chair. Crossing her slender waxed legs, a porcelain demitasse of espresso appeared at her left elbow. An appreciative sip told her this was not synth but a rare authentic blend.

ESAIC Blake sat facing her on the same side of the table. They were knee-to-knee. Blake's familiarity unnerved her, but he was a gentleman in all other respects.

"Madame Proconsul, I am honored by your visit. My old

partner Harley is your father? How delightful! You seek trust and discretion. How may I help you?"

"Agent Blake, you are perceptive. Please call me Libby. Kind of you to see me. Time is of the essence. I am in over my head and I need your help." She surprised herself at how difficult that came out, even now. She rehearsed that all the way from Maryginia.

"Tell me what you think I might offer, Libby."

"I'm sponsoring a piece of legislation that is aggressively lobbied by some large business concerns. New information came to me that if this bill becomes policy, we will witness, well, adverse effects from its implementation. They could be widespread, and may even present a public health hazard."

"Forgive my ignorance of all things political, Libby. But if you are this bill's sponsor for which you now seem to harbor doubts, why not just abort the bill before it comes to a vote? Is that the proper terminology?"

She squirmed her slender bottom and adjusted her crossed legs. She now wished she had worn a longer skirt. "Allow me to clarify. I believe my life is in danger and am no longer needed to get the bill passed. It seems I may be a... loose end. Is that not a term? Certain business concerns— backers of this bill—possess incredible resources. In return for my support, they were backing my bid for magister. That is no longer possible. They kill people, Agent Blake."

"Edmond, please. Libby, I must ask hard questions if I am to help you, although I'm still not clear what you would ask of me."

"Please. I need discretion and advice from an old friend of the family. Off the record. Ask away."

"Who are 'they?'"

"Carmen Rios of the Grandy Group, Mayfield Bailey of Gray and Foster Telecom Consulting, an influential lobbying firm in New Wash, and Anderson Dean of the Capitol Security Service. There may be others, but those are the three with whom I am acquainted."

"To what health hazard do you refer, Libby?"

"Well, some speak of an intensified EMP danger, at least those who subscribe to theories of emerging scientific research. But I just learned this morning of something else with which I cannot abide. I do not believe I was to discover this until after my bill passed into policy, if ever. Learning of two treasonous initiatives enabled by my bill appalled me and spurred me into action. Revealing this may cost me my career. I no longer care. But I would like to survive."

"You have my complete attention. What are these two initiatives, Libby."

After she described her understanding of TESS and TEMP, she said, "So am I a paranoid lunatic, Edmond?"

"We have heard rumors. You've provided us useful corroboration of those rumors. We will interview Mr. Rios, Mr. Bailey, and Mr. Dean."

Madame Proconsul's legendary poker face had folded upon entering his office. She was a portrait of transparency. Now her face became a mask of fear. Agent Blake could not miss her visceral reaction.

"We will be discreet. For now, can you tell me anything else that you feel might be useful?"

LIBBY BLADE HESITATED AS AGENT BLAKE WAITED. IT SEEMED her voluntary interview might transition into an interrogation. She should have a lawyer present, but she *was* a lawyer. This had already gone too far. Now Madame Proconsul saw no way out. As she sat in Edmond Blake's office, a friend of the family, but also one of the top AIA agents in the

Alliance, she saw only one option: to relieve herself of the rest of the story. So she said, "I am no scientist. But there is evidence to suggest a massive cloud of satellites, once transmitting 10G telecom signals at full strength, could a linchpin to disrupt the earth's magnetosphere. Are you familiar with this concept, Edmond?"

"I am."

"And are you aware of what such a disruption could mean to global integrity?"

"Yes, Libby."

Her concern deepened. Blake knew of the magnetosphere *and* its devastating effects on the planet if disrupted. Further, he exhibited no shock over her revealing news of a likely extinction event if her legislation passed into policy. Quite the contrary, he seemed calm and rather pleased with himself. What was going on here?

"Edmond, this is old news to you. Am I reading you?"

"You are."

"***And...?***" Now her demeanor skittered somewhere between exasperation and panic.

"Before I answer you, is there anything else you wish to share with me, Libby?"

Her voice flattened, her eyelids squinted and wrinkled. "No, I can think of nothing else."

Edmond said, "Some people believe in God, some in fate. Some might call what's happening here serendipity. Subject to our investigation, which has been underway for some time, it is fortuitous you are here today, Libby. You have not only aided in furthering our case by volunteering key information, you have exonerated yourself on charges of high treason. Until today, we would have charged you for your treasonous role in this affair. I am delighted the daughter of my old partner is not a traitor. While you will face charges for other crimes, treason was the primary. Libby, it is also serendipitous you will not be leaving here today. Our inquiries suggest a conspiracy of wider scope than you have revealed or imagined. You are in mortal danger. You *are* a loose end. There is no doubt. You will be safe here. For that, I am glad."

She went slack. Her arms fell to her sides as she sat. "I'm under... arrest?"

"No, Madame Proconsul, we are not charging you. But you are a person of interest in several murders. You are free to go as I do not consider you a flight risk, but I would recommend against that. I also recommend you retain the services of an attorney. But for now, I suggest you remain our guest."

Blake's words stunned her. This was not how she saw this day evolving. From valiant whistleblower to a suspected felon in less than an hour!

A stern young man in a beautiful pinstripe suit entered the office. ESAIC Blake directed his remarks to him. "Agent Rantelli, Ms. Blade is here to help with an investigation. She is also a person of interest with whom we'll want to conduct an extended interview, so she is our guest. Please offer her every courtesy. Ensure she is comfortable in our executive interview room for now. Provide her access to refreshments and to as many voxcons as she may require." Now addressing his remarks back to her, he said, "Libby, I advise you not to disclose your location to anyone. A precaution for your safety. We'll talk again."

And that was that. The polite young man held the portal open for her. Libby needed time to think, anyway. In safety. It seemed they had now given her the opportunity to do so. A frightened but arrogant prima donna entered Agent Blake's office. A wounded zombie shuffled out.

Interrogations did not often amuse Agent Blake, and there was nothing amusing about the atrocities his old partner's daughter attempted to mount against the Alliance. For what? Money? Power?

Despite her demure demeanor, Libby Blade might not be a traitor, but she was a cold-blooded killer.

32

N EW WASH,
MARYGINIA

THE FINAL BRIEFING AT ONE ALLIANCE PLAZA IN CHICAGO
with ESAIC Blake of the AIA told Zaya everything he
needed to hear. He was clear to publish his exclusive uncen-
sored report, except no mention of magnetosphere stuff.
Libby Blade, Proconsul of the Assembly of Elders of the
United Westican Territories, would testify to her role in the
conspiracy to commit five murders. And to her unwitting
role in facilitating the Grandy Group's strategy to weaponize
EMP. With her help, killing the bill to enable that became a
fait accompli.

Zaya and Lamatte said their goodbyes to Detective
Lionel Smith and Captain Judge Miners. After the twenty-
five minute flight from the O Tower in Chicago to Bethesda,
Lamatte went his own way. Zaya looked forward to a long
night's sleep in his neglected transport in the New Wash

exurbs.

Lamatte insisted Zaya take custody of his tiny pulse weapon, the one with which he once held Zaya at bay, and the one that saved him from certain death at the hands of two SS assassins outside his transport before going to Chicago. Seemed so long ago. Lamatte now thought Zaya needed it more. *Does he know something?*

Lamatte said, "I'm no longer a target, but you might be. Just trust me, okay my friend?"

So Zaya was armed. He wasn't comfortable carrying a weapon, but his friend asked for his trust. How could he find fault in that?

While Zaya caught a local to his rig, Lamatte caught another to St. Vroman's Sacred Heart Rectory, on AIA's tab. Somewhat evasive, Lamatte hinted of 'an appointment with destiny.' The man was in love. He would no longer deny it. The notion consumed him. Zaya felt nothing but warmth in his heart for his only real friend, except for one Chicago cop, and now his beautiful boss. Oh, and a girl who lived in a tunnel, but that was much more than friendship.

The sight of his rig sent a thrill drilling through the pit of his stomach. Too long away—four entire days. An eternity. His device vibrated against his chest and the tingle from his skin-bud announced an incoming voxcon.

Zaya pressed his breast pocket just as the transport's steps swished out to greet him. He took two steps up to peer into the optical recognition lock, amazed it deciphered his eye-print as bloodshot as it must be. His mind reeled from a lack of sleep and a lightning round of events in the Windy City. As the portal swished open, he entered his cherished home that was festooned with thrusters and wheels and jacks. And memories.

"Hallo…" That was his exhausted version of *hello*. "*PGirl?*"

"Zaya! You're entering your transport!"

"Um, yeah. I know."

"Get out! Get out now! Run! A bomb! *Go, go, go!*

Shit! Dropped his duffel. Spun off-balance on his heels. Stumbled. Caught himself on the grab rail to his right as he faced the still-open portal from the cockpit. Saw the Restful Acres RV Resort out there. Entered a slow-motion nightmare. A dream of no pain engulfed him. He'd likely be dead before his nerve endings could process, well, anything. Then, he pulled free from the molasses. Threw himself from the transport. He tumbled down the steps to the hardpan ground. Crawled with desperation. He so wanted to live. He wanted to see PodGirl again. Needed to feel her love before his mind cast him into a flesh-shredding darkness. Got up to run and—

Whump!

Seconds later, the flames gave substance to the heavy haze hanging over Restful Acres. A total lack of sound puzzled Zaya as he swam in a sea of clumpy confusion. The blast had thrown him five yards before he came to rest against the wall of the dilapidated mag-pull trailer east of his rig. The old-fashioned alumasteel frame-and-sheath construction of his now-decarcassed twenty-year-old transport had contained much of the blast. *I must still be alive.* The confusion became less oppressive and noisier after several moments. Curious, a few residents approached to investigate and to offer help. *If it hadn't been for PodGirl's voxcon....*

Then he sensed a malignant presence. Twenty yards away, a hulking figure approached, scaring off the Good Samaritans. A massive silhouette materialized between Zaya and the flames. Someone whispered: *Zaya, find that little weapon in your right coat pocket. Now!*

It was *so* unlike Zaya to carry something like that. He could not overlook the irony that an ex-priest forced that weapon on him less than a half-hour ago. Now ten yards away, the edges of that silhouette sharpened, darkened. A mission-worthy march in this hulk's gait signaled he was no friend. Not an innocent bystander. Nor was this a Good Samaritan.

As he drew closer, Zaya could make out a mountain of a man with huge hands hanging nearly to his knees. He radiated a malevolent aura. Those gorilla hands clenched and unclenched as he shuffled toward Zaya's still-prone remains. The silhouette meant to extinguish what life still stirred in his target. When the hulk was less than two yards from Zaya's feet, he paused. Heard his voice. "You survive, little big man. I change that now. It's a job."

Garlic and whiskey Retif Zlatan? From the *gym*? Zaya's mind became that of a cheesy game show host: *We have a winner! And the grand prize is a pulse weapon. You can use this handy little device for any number of purposes. But the top choice by our studio audience is to shoot in the forehead any asshole who may try to assassinate you! Now SPIN THAT WHEEL, PILGRIM!*

Zaya gripped the little weapon in his fist, still inside his pocket. As Zaya drew his hand out of his pocket and raised his right arm, Retif's eyes widened in recognition. He rushed to crush his target with his weight and to render the weapon useless.

Too late. The crackle of lightning and the smell of ozone combined with that of burning bacon fat hit Zaya's nose after that monster fell on his legs, his journey to Zaya's chest abbreviated by destiny. Then, nothing but smoke and fog and....

CHAOS....

Zaya didn't hear the asynchronous bee-bah-bee-bah of two competing sirens as they grew close. A pair of transports hovered low into the RV park—one policy enforcement and one fire. Both approached the burning wreckage of his transport, along with another small trailer west of it, collapsed and smoldering.

Unconsciousness spared Zaya another painful sight: mangled remnants of his custom Road Commander's frame pinned against the nearby perimeter fence. The explosion's concussive force scattered a few other larger parts of his precious motorcycle around a good portion of Restful Acres.

A trio of NWFD first responders—medders—stood over him seconds later while others contained the fire's fury by projecting a flame-retardant shield. The medders stared for a beat at a huge corpse sprawled at a diagonal across Zaya's bloody legs. They then assessed a cauterized hole the diameter of a child's wrist through the corpse's huge skull. Zaya sensed more than heard their inquisitive banter as they rolled the monster off their victim and administered first aid to *the live one.*

"How could an anonymous voxcon from *Chicago* have been so specific with the precise location and description of this guy? The dispatcher even mentioned a second larger victim, wounded or dead, but if not dead, to consider him armed and dangerous."

"What in Hell is going on here?"

"Let's just do what we can for the live one and be grateful we didn't have to deal with *that* one."

33

———————

B ETHESDA, MARYGINIA

ZAYA AWAKENED. HE SPOTTED A HOODED FIGURE SITTING IN A chair as far away as possible from the only window in the hospital room. Sierra rose to stand beside his bed. The hood stayed up with her mask in place, but she kissed his right cheek. Then came the embrace, but she was still just standing there by the bed, a yard distant.

This will take some getting used to, but what a wonderful way to return from death. I did die, didn't I?

Even though flat on his back, attached to a variety of machines, Sierra climbed in beside him. At first, her touch was feather light, fearing she might hurt him. She conformed to his shape, exercising care not to touch him below the waist or above his eyes.

"You're warm. So warm."

He only felt... cold. Once again she sensed what Zaya

needed. Her fingers wandered around his neck and right cheek, but always stopped halfway up his face.

Sierra said, "They bandaged your head, dear heart. You suffered a severe concussion. But you're alive. And we're together. Isn't this friendship-turned-to-love thing amazing?"

"Yeah... still, the fog... amazing... warm, but cold... Other things?"

"Later. Sleep. With me."

LATER CAME. THREE DAYS LATER. ZAYA'S MEDICATION regimen continued as he clarified his thoughts. He needed more information, even amidst his residual confusion. Sierra stayed with him the entire time. Even consumed by her fear of exposure, and the chaotic noise that disturbed her most, she stayed, for him. She told him not to worry. She tried to convince him a few days of exposure wouldn't kill her. Not with her lace garments and a tight copper fabric hood like medieval chainmail under a more conventional sweatshirt hood. Said she was okay. Add the shielded mask and goggles, even indoors, and bolstered by Birdman's anti-chaos medication, Sierra would do what was necessary to stay close to *her man.*

He guessed she wore her goggles high on her forehead at the moment only so he could see the affection oozing from her hazelnut eyes. The entire affectation reminded him of an early twentieth-century aviation pioneer with a few contemporary upgrades. She was such a very different person up here. Finally, Sierra collapsed from exhaustion and stress in the chair at his bedside—far away from the window. He feared for her. Zaya sensed she was a smoldering mess. *She must really love me! And what she now means to me? I can't imagine being away from her.*

Zaya gazed at his Pgirl, sitting there sleeping, but didn't see a cloak, a hood, or the unnecessary mask. He only saw his beautiful guardian angel, his soulmate. Soulmate? A tired cliché he'd summarily reject in his writing, but he now kept it close to his heart. Yes, convinced beyond any shadow of doubt or insecurity, he had found his soulmate, corny or not.

God, he just wanted to pull out all the stupid needles. He needed to escape this stupid bed, to rush over to her little huddled form with her legs tucked under. She hugged herself as if to minimize her exposure. He needed to smother her with every thread of his being. He wished he were made of copper fabric to shield her with his body from real or imagined hazards. But they had strapped him to this bed.

Just then, her eyes popped open. She cast them in his direction.

Did I awaken her?

She thought, *It's okay, dear heart.* She switched to speech. "Zaya, I wanted to be the one to tell you, in private. Your injuries will surprise you. More than that, you need to know how important you are to me, that you are alive. That is our priority."

Still in a half-dream state, Zaya said, "As long as we're together..." But he steeled himself for the bad news she was about to deliver.

"You've lost your right leg and your left arm, dear heart. Shrapnel."

She let that sink in. He said nothing. Thought nothing.

"Because I called 911 *before* I called to warn you, they

arrived just as the explosion took place, found you in less than a minute, and applied emergency aid."

"I have one arm, and one leg." Not a question, but adjusting to a new normal, he imagined. Seemed trivial. He was just so very pissed off.

She said, "Yes. But you'll walk, and you'll write—even better than before—with auto-prosthetics, they tell me. Think of the story potential!" He didn't need the ability to *do that thing* to sense the contrived optimism in her voice.

He annoyed himself that his next notion even occurred to him. "You saved my life, Sierra, but why did you voxcon instead of just, um, doing your thing?"

"It's called telepathy, or telepathic communication, dear heart. I sensed that your voxcon response time would be quicker. You are more accustomed to voxcons. And it's okay to wonder about that. I'm still wondering how I knew. Well, it doesn't matter. I was topside. Already on my way to you."

Because telepathy came easier to Sierra than words, he just thought, *What now?*

"Well, you heal, we get your new arm and leg installed, we spend some time in rehab, and you come live with me in The Digs! We can both podcast to our hearts' content, or not. Does that work for you?"

'We' feels right to me. Yes, that works. Oh God, what am I doing? What have I become? I'm only half a man now. What aren't you telling me, my sweet?

Before she could respond to reassure him, his heart rate doubled, his blood pressure plummeted, his eyes rolled to pure white, and the monitors went crazy.

A NURSE RUSHED IN. IT ASKED SIERRA TO LEAVE THE ROOM AS it shouted into its integrated comms for Doctor Somebody-or-other and ordered an emergency kit of some sort.

Sierra knew to disappear. Zaya needed further urgent attention that she didn't understand. But he would be alright. She'd tell him about his other injuries after he stabilized. The important part of him survived—his mind. Most of it, anyway. He would need time. And she'd be close, with her copper lace and hood and mask and goggles and meds and attitude. Until they could get home. Safe. Together.

Nobody in the odious waiting room could observe Sierra's sunshine smile. They saw a mask that made her face below her eyes look like a naked skull with protruding cheek bones—small twin O2 tricklers. Her curse had become her gift. She felt gratitude. For her completeness. Their wholeness.

She attracted a few stares. A middle-aged man appeared both overweight and emaciated, like a half-bloated, half-empty skin bag whose contents settled below his waist. His bug eyes atop tiny shoulders stared at her, and she thought *he* should be the patient, not waiting for his wife of forty years to die. Poor thing.

A younger woman judged Sierra with silly thoughts of how her strange appearance spoke to her obvious inferiority, but Sierra did not resent her. The bigoted woman lingered to see if her son would survive his accident.

So much raucous noise!

They stared, not because of her macabre mask, maybe because she chose not to sit on a chair, but cross-legged on a table in a far corner. She was sure they stared as they watched her darting gaze, looking at nothing. Sierra had moved the stack of magazine tablets from the end table to a nearby chair. She then roosted and huddled on that little corner table with her head lowered. Just so. These frogs could see she had chosen the life of a bird, but could not understand why. To each their own. Now she just needed to rest between the lighter green beams, to manage the cacophony, and to wait.

At last, the time came for her next conversation with her dear Zaya. He used to be her height at five-and-a-half feet. Now she imagined he felt smaller. Or less. Still a giant, a man of substance, of courage. He was fearless and persistent. He would be okay. He had to be okay.

Zaya said, "You've been here the whole time." Not a question.

"Where else would I be? Besides, it's only been only a week. Birdman pretends to wonder why I'm here, but he knows. Yesterday he said one future has arrived, and it includes us. He asks if you'll join our community, that you are welcome if you wish it."

"He can't *do that thing,* distant telepathy, with me?"

"Zaya, you and I share a strong connection. He shares such connections with others, including me, but not with you. Yet. It's complicated. Up close, he's very good with everyone who allows it. He must be selective, you can imagine."

"Well, to his offer, it seems I am now homeless. I would like to try life in The Digs. But I'm not yet sure about living underground longer term. More than anything, though, I want us to be together. Anywhere. So, yes. Absolutely. To live with a bunch of telepaths? I'll need some time to adjust, won't I?"

"Not everyone in The Digs is a tellie. Folks will adjust to you too. Um, let's talk injuries, okay?"

"Sure. No right leg and no left arm. Awkward since I'm left-handed. What else?" He sounded more cavalier than he felt.

"Your doctors agreed you'd get the summary from me. Zaya, you died.

"I think I knew that."

"The first responders restarted your heart after almost a minute of resuscitation. I felt you die, you sweet man. We took that brief journey that lasted an eternity. Together. I hitch-hiked. Oh, Zaya, we spent that eternity in each other's arms. You drifted on such a soft cloud it tempted me to let you float away, but my selfish heart didn't want to lose you. I asked you to come back, to *this*," she passed her hand over the flat bed where his leg should have been, "and you came back with me!" Tears rolled down both her cheeks onto her mask. "You love me more than—"

"Shut up, PodGirl. You brought me back from death. I sure could use a real kiss."

Off came the mask. He wrapped his only arm around the back of her neck to draw her in. After a long slow kiss, salty with tears, she lay her head on his wrapped chest. Neither words nor mental images came easy, but he needed to know the rest now.

Once again, she knew what he needed. "Zaya, your spleen ruptured when you hit that trailer. The good news? That old trailer wall caved in and absorbed much of the impact. The bad news? No more spleen. That just means your immune system will weaken as a result, so you must take certain lifestyle precautions. Living in The Digs will help."

His voice grew flat, his thoughts grew darker. "That it?"

He was shutting down, but she forged ahead. He needed to know it all. Sierra tried to keep her voice and the rest of her demeanor light, yet earnest, but she could not hide the slight wavering of her voice. She gripped his only hand as if she could never let it go. "You suffered a severe traumatic brain injury, but now with the swelling receding, your cognitive processes seem fine. There could be symptoms later, but they seem pleased. That's it, or so I'm told. Oh, Zaya...." Sierra did not say such a TBI might affect her ability to share his thoughts, or that his mental state could change. But they had today, and maybe tomorrow. Maybe the day after. Maybe more.

"It's okay, Sweetheart. One day at a time. We'll worry about tomorrow and my mental state later. When can we go home?"

Sierra's eyes widened, *Could it be?* But then she relaxed,

With their heads together, they cried more silent tears of gratitude. Together.

34

NEW WASH, MARYGINIA

IT SEEMED DOOMSDAY HAD BEEN STALLED, AT LEAST FOR NOW. Four months after Lucy Candelson's funeral, her parents accepted the Magisterial Medal of Freedom on their daughter's behalf. This highest civilian award was also presented to Madeleine Haley's son for his mother by the grateful magister of the United Westica Territories.

After completing the initial phase of a nationwide Department of Judgement investigation, spearheaded by the Alliance Intelligence Agency, they convicted Libby Blade of conspiracy to commit murder, sentenced to life in the Cuban Penal Colony. She got her wish. She survived.

They posthumously convicted Retif Zlatan on five counts of first degree murder including the heinous death of the Secretary Haley. CED Captain Judge Miners closed her case.

Anderson Dean was also convicted posthumously for high treason and for an act of terrorism resulting in the deaths of Libby Blade's staff.

An Alliance grand jury convicted Grandy Group's Carmen Rios and GFTC's Mayfield Bailey of treason, sedition, and conspiracy to commit murder. Convictions as accessories before, concurrent, or after the fact, of several associates followed. Sentencing was pending.

Libby's daughter, Sierra, corresponded with her mother at least once a month. In one of those communiques, Libby shared with her that Mayfield Bailey succumbed to wounds suffered during a brutal attack by fellow CPC inmates. Sierra would later learn that Bailey—along with another gentleman named Dean, also deceased—was a party to the attacks on both her and her mother. Sierra could guess what her mother meant when she said, "Who says I don't know how to clean house?"

Grandy's CEO, Camille Apollinaire, took control of her research and development programs with an iron fist. She felt the need to over-compensate for her CFO's corruption. Besides, the AIA's investigation of her company's operations would keep its activities under close scrutiny for years to come. Ms. Apollinaire commissioned a comprehensive light frequency communication and energy transfer program with billions in R&D funding. She also committed to a sweeping ten-year strategy and its implementation to that technology. LF would become the cleaner alternative to its dirtier ray-spraying radio frequency counterpart. Ms. Apollinaire also vowed Grandy would phase out all RF products and services within twenty years. The climatology communities applauded her position.

THE NWPD AND AIA GRILLED A CANTANKEROUS OLD PRIEST for his subversive communiques with one of his parishioners, Carmen Rios. While they chose not to charge him with a policy violation, they informed his Bishop that he had violated his sacred vows.

Further, they informed the bitter old Jesuit of the significant recognition bestowed upon Lamatte Foliére by the Chicago Enforcement Department and the Alliance Intelligence Agency. They then released Father Benedict Scolario on his own recognizance. He remained skeptical. And bitter. And alone. And ex-communicated. To the end of his days. He drank himself to death.

The *Grandy Calamity,* as a small circle of New Wash insiders would remember it, fueled the righteous indignation of pious politicians to investigate and indict everyone but themselves.

After a peaceful transition of power, the new UWT magister assured the Westican people a sustained focus on rooting out widespread greed and corruption in New Wash and across the Alliance, as well as within the ranks of its international big business collaborators. United Westicans would remember Madame Magister's first term for its melee of circuitous investigations that ground her administration and the entire UWT political process to a ponderous crawl.

35

THE DIGS BENEATH OLD CHICAGO

SANCTUARY! LAMATTE FOLIÉRE AND MARIA GUTIERREZ sought refuge from surface clutter with Birdman and his subterranean flock. Zaya French sought the same so he could be with his beloved PodGirl—Sierra Blade. All were welcome. Birdman, an ordained Methodist minister from a previous life, officiated at a double wedding for the Frenches and the Foliéres.

Residents of The Digs invited and guided the new CED Chief of Detectives, Chief Judge Miners, and her new deputy, Captain Lionel Smith, to the affair. Both policy officers were welcomed as their innermost affection for their newest community members required no words and offered no deception.

Chief Miners saw first-hand how The Digs self-policied their community. She was quick to declare it *Restricted Terri-*

tory in recognition of Birdman's and Sierra's contributions to solving the Haley case, not to mention their contributions to the AIA's broader series of investigations. This meant The Digs—this unique and wonderful place—would remain out-of-bounds from a policy enforcement perspective. This restriction would endure through Chief Detective Miners' eventual tenure as CED's Chief of Policy Enforcement and later, as the Chicago Policy Commissioner.

Birdman, the unofficial mayor of The Digs now basked in the friendship and protection of their new topside friends in high places.

BUT TIME PLAGUED BIRDMAN'S WAKING VISIONS AND HIS dreams—when he was able to sleep. More than he could control. He saw the Grandy Calamity as something different —a harbinger for the demise of politics. Effective global leadership would not surface until the world endured several years of bloody transitions. Beyond that, yet another transition loomed. Nothing would be the same. Nothing. But ultimately, nobody would mind.

He craved contrast. Balance. Cross-legged on his rag rug, weeks after welcoming the trio of topsiders to his community, Birdman meditated in his apartment. He battled a malevolent spirit, its awareness awakened by his new partnership with these topsiders. A new ripple.

Birdman's torment sustained his precious purpose—contrast and balance. Without black, nothing but white meant oblivion. Just white. And without white, only darkness.

He would not deny certain inevitabilities. Evil existed in this world, maybe in all worlds, providing necessary contrast. So be it. His gift—or curse—coerced him to extract future probabilities from their unmolested timelines, forcing him to acknowledge them in the present, to be guided by them. The end game had begun, and he identified his role in it. Or rather, that of his estranged son's pivotal role.

Individual issues, like self-induced radiation poisoning, loss of the ozone layer, less breathable air, and poisoned oceans weren't the problems. They were but symptoms. Humanity remained bent on its own destruction.

His vision's inevitability brought a certain tranquility to Birdman's torment. Not in his lifetime, but during his children's, he foresaw the possibility of an upgrade to all life. *UpLife! They have but to choose. It is theirs to lose. Or win.*

It is not done...

Note: While the concept of electromagnetic poisoning presented in "Mayhem: Underground" may sound like a bizarre fictional concept, serious science has forced many researchers around the world to consider this a potential mass health hazard. For more information, see ***www.5gSpaceAppeal.org***

APPENDIX A - CAST
OF MAJOR CHARACTERS

In alphabetical order:

- **Camille Apollinaire:** Grandy Group's CEO.
- **Mayfield Bailey:** New Wash lobbyist and sole proprietor of Gray and Foster Telecom Consulting, whose exclusive client is the Grandy Group.
- **Birdman:** see Fen Morrissee.
- **Elizabeth (Libby) Blade:** Montanaho Proconsulwoman of the 28th Assembly of Elders for the United Westican Territories.
- **Sierra Blade:** a.k.a. PodGirl, estranged daughter of Libby Blade and resident of The Digs.
- **Edmond Blake:** Executive Special Agent in Charge, Midwestern Headquarters of the Alliance Intelligence Agency (AIA), successor to the Federal Bureau of Investigation in Old America.

- **Lucy Candelson:** One of Libby Blade's aides within the Assembly of Elders.
- **Anderson Dean:** Supervisory Agent within the Capitol Security Service.
- **Father Lamatte Foliére:** Volunteer at the Georgetown University Research Library and Reading Room; Jesuit priest in residence at St. Vroman's Sacred Heart Church in New Wash.
- **Isaiah (Zaya) French:** Author, journalist, storyteller, podcaster, and unofficial crime fighter.
- **Maria Gutierrez:** Sister Maria of St. Vroman's Church.
- **Madeleine Haley:** United Westica's Secretary of Defense.
- **Seamus Harstow:** A Grandy Group business policy executive.
- **Judge Miners:** Captain, Chicago Enforcement Department (CED) and Smitty's boss.
- **Fen Morrissee:** aka **Birdman**, unofficial mayor of The Digs under Old Chicago, Williana. **Seer.** Lay minister. Father of twin daughters (Cherry and Strawberry) as well as a son, Joshua, who lives with relatives.
- **Carmen Rios:** The Grandy Group's Chief Financial Officer.
- **Father Benedict Scolario:** Father Lamatte Foliére's fellow parish priest and confessor at St. Vroman's Sacred Heart Church and rectory.
- **Lionel Smith:** a.k.a. Smitty, Detective, Chicago Enforcement Department (CED)
- **Retif Zlatan:** Hired thug employed by Anderson Dean of the Capitol Security Service.

APPENDIX B - RELATIONSHIP
MAP OF CHARACTERS

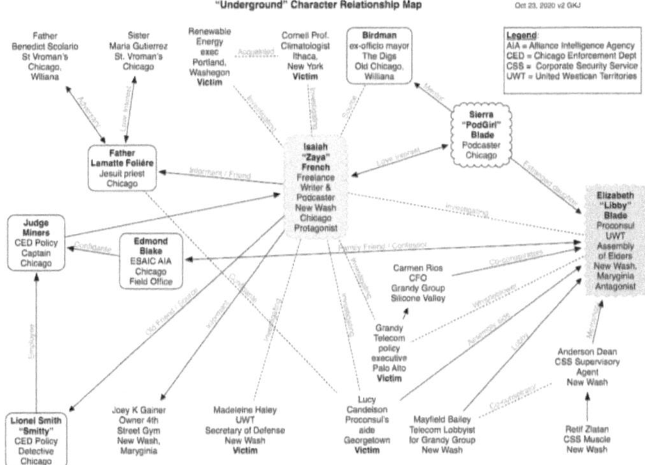

APPENDIX C - GLOSSARY

And now a reference for the language of Westica from the years 2148 to 2150.

In alphabetical order:

- **Birds:** Folks whose lifestyle defines them. Birds are consumed by fear of health hazards caused by electromagnetic—EM—radiation. If they don't live underground or in highly shielded conditions, they believe EM rays will poison them.
- **Cages:** Shielding that birds use to avoid EM radiation. Most popular shielding comprises metal, metallic screening or natural earth. Copper fabric hoods and clothing helps. Some birds even line their masks with copper fabric.
- **Casters:** Short for *broadcasters*, those who use electronics and telecommunications media to broadcast.

- **EMP:** Electromagnetic pollution or EM poisoning, an unintended consequence of emerging telecommunications technologies.
- **Frogs:** Topsiders who remain oblivious to the dangers of EMP (aka ray spray). Like frogs sitting comfortably in warm water, as the temperature increases, they boil to death without realizing the danger.
- **Headlights (aka goggles):** Renders high-power microwave-frequency electromagnetic waves (aka rays) visible to the human eye.
- **Islands:** Non-telepathic individuals (they are *islands* unto themselves).
- **Lace:** Body cages that enclose vital organs and appendages with metallic fabric.
- **Nayers:** Nihilistic naysaying birds who accept, even welcome, the logical conclusion of the frogs' destructive proclivities. Nayers predict the end of days approaches. They believe frogs unwittingly embrace not only their own destruction, but everyone's.
- **Nolos:** Low- or no-income folks.
- **Puters:** Once called computers. Various form factors from desktop, laptop, handheld, wristpad, or implant (left temple).
- **Rays** (aka ray spray): Electromagnetic rays that may or may not be harmful to flora or fauna. Birds believe harmful rays (those above a certain frequency and power threshold) correlate to an array of symptoms such as headaches, growths and sundry disorders such as confusion, depression, and disorientation. The afflicted can keep no food down, even when it's available.

- **Regionplexes:** Sprawling urban areas that emerged as metroplexes grew to cover entire regions of United Westica. They typically extended hundreds of miles in every direction.
- **Tellies:** Folks who possess telepathic skills
- **Topsiders:** Folks or animals who live on the surface (not underground). They live *topside*.
- **Tricklers:** Automatic oxygen delivery devices often integrated into face masks.
- **Tweeners:** Topsiders who admit to living in fear of ray spray are unfortunates who live in denial. They choose to take precautions, but will never likely complete their transition from living topside.
- **Vidcons:** two-way video connections, or conferences that can include any number of participants through their implanted or external devices.
- **Vidcords:** video recordings made through implanted or external devices.
- **Voxconn:** a two-way audio connection they used to refer to as a telephone call.
- **Exurbs:** Those nether regions between urban neighborhoods and the suburbs.

ALSO BY GK JURRENS

Take a peek at a preview of *"Mayhem: Mean Streets,"* thirteen years after *"Mayhem: Underground,"* where you'll once again encounter Birdman, Zaya, Lamatte and some new compatriots during the advent of Westica's second civil war as a backdrop.

Birdman, our reluctant visionary, sends Zaya, Sierra and Lamatte on a quest to influence three obscure events or risk planetary extinction.

The world can be cruel, but hope emerges within the United Westican Territories of the 2160s during a bloody civil war.

Journalist Zaya French and his telepathic wife Sierra partner once again with the gifted Lamatte Foliére and their old friend, the new Chicago Chief of Detectives, their old friend, Lionel Smith, a.k.a. *Smitty*.

Zaya, Sierra and Lamatte thrive in a subterranean sanctuary called The Digs beneath the sprawling regionplex of Chicago, Williana, under the leadership of an enigmatic seer known only as Birdman.

Smitty recruits his drop-dead-gorgeous boss, Policy Commissioner Judge Miners, and her well-placed political friends to help these renegades rescue their nation's future, and maybe all of humanity's.

Turmoil reaches abysmal proportions in the streets of the UWT, from coast to coast, and from tundra to cape. Worse, *global* political governance has failed. Something must be done, and normal citizens are called upon to take action.

But how can our small group succeed in their trio of pivotal quests against countless professional assassins and armed paramilitary groups roaming the streets who constantly collide with combat soldiers ill-trained for urban warfare?

Prepare for a rough ride. 2163 Chicago—ground zero—is the most dangerous city in the world. But it's home.

Turn the page for an excerpt of "Mayhem: Mean Streets"

EXCERPT - MAYHEM: MEAN STREETS

—

DIRTY MONEY

New Wash, Maryginia
United Westican Territories (UWT)
August 2163

Their voices warbled as they conspired. "Look, you'll get your money. Just get it done." Both of their comm implants enabled end-to-end encryption and decryption of their conversation. It also disguised their voices. This comprised their only acquaintance with each other besides vaulted access codes for such voxcons and anonymous, extra-continental accounts. They both believed it would stay that way.

"Hey, shut up and listen, you pompous politician! I want double. After tomorrow, if I'm still alive, I'll need to leave the continent. Forever. And our expenses ran far higher than expected to orchestrate this little party of yours."

"That is not our problem. He expects results. Disappointment will not be acceptable. Do you want him as an enemy? You know what he does to those who dare take advantage of him."

The connection went quiet. The warbling susurrus of burst-transmission encryption should have provided the caller a stronger sense of security. It didn't.

"All right, fine. But listen, I need protection. Even in the non-extradition haven where I'm headed. I need personal assurances. My crew, however, is on their own."

"That will not be a problem. The proconsul takes care of his friends. But remember, he also finds and deals harshly with his enemies, *wherever* they may scurry. I trust we have an understanding. And make sure that ridiculous flag is visible during the attack."

Swish.

BIRDMAN'S BATTLE

The Digs
  Under Old Chicago,
  Williana

Always the same, and always different, solitude helped, if he could find it. But solitude proved illusory. Molten knives stabbed Birdman's eyes, teased of abating, but did not. Closed-mouth screams layered onto whispered shouts of muttered desperation, of professed love, of certain death.

Yes, it all came to him, even the deep-exhale surrenders of those expiring as they crossed the final dark line of that profound transitory event. Strange, but those dark crossings clutched at his pain centers the least, as they, unlike the others, offered a lightness, a final unbounded freedom. But all the others...

*She loves me.... That's a lie.... He hates us!.... The best day of my life.... Cinnamon, sage, boiled cabbage.... I hate you.... Something's very wrong.... So wonderful.... My eyes—the burning—can't breathe!.... Please don't die!.... I'll do anything... Shots fired/officer down/how many?/**aghhhh!***

Birdman's intense yellow eyes looked like they would burn a hole through the glass of the only window in his small apartment. The boy followed his mentor's intense gaze, only seeing the flame of a huge candle resting on a small table near the cracked and peeling window sill.

"Sir? Are you okay? Sir!"

And suddenly, those deep-set dark eyes twinkled with warmth and immediacy once again. Like before.

"Sorry? Oh, now where and when were we? Ah, yes. Be patient. You must remain positive and hopeful, even during dark times. This moment is *your* moment, no one else's. Now finish your tea and go ask her, like we rehearsed. All right, m'boy?"

He smiled at the shiny young man punishing the few soft chin hairs on which he unconsciously tugged. There were so few young ones.

Birdman also smiled at the wonder of the indomitable human spirit and of innocent adolescent infatuation. But most of all, he smiled because he so needed to cherish this moment, unsure of how many more in which he would be privileged to indulge.

"Um, thank you, sir. You're the best."

"No, thank *you*, m'boy, for reminding me how precious every breath of life should be, every thought, every emotion. Now forget the tea you're just pretending to enjoy. Go find her and ask her. Right this moment. Go!"

After a brief homage to his mentor, the boy sprang for the door before he had thoroughly untangled his spindly legs. He tripped on the frayed edge of the ragged old rug upon which they sat. The partially filled teacup at his feet upended with a tinkle and a splash. He stumbled, cast an embarrassing glance over his shoulder at the wide-grinning Birdman, and mumbled, "Sorry...." as he grabbed the ancient brass knob.

The warped portal stuck and creaked as the boy jerked it open against some protest. It was actual wood, a rare commodity possessed of endearing quirks. Wood seemed happiest when being worked. That door remained closed more than not.

Birdman bathed himself in a warm glow as he heard the boy clomp down the narrow stairs, also wooden, also creaking with delight. Like a puppy whose feet were too big, he would be a tall one.

Puppies. A distant memory... from before.

And then it began anew, but with less scat...

What would Birdman say?... I love this place... will I ever be with child?... need a trip to the lower tunnels to fetch water... will you trade a head of cabbage for two carrots?....

———

TOUGH STREETS

Chicago, Williana
    August 2163

Time and crime mocked Policy Enforcement in this sprawling population center.

The largest regionplex in the United Westican Territories, Chicago encompassed the geographic area from what was once called Madison, Wisconsin to Indianapolis, Indiana, and south of Springfield, Illinois in Old America.

There was every good reason the CED—Chicago Enforcement Department—was the largest policy enforcement organization in the world.

En route to ground zero for one of tonight's many festivities, CED prowlers screamed close overhead in near silence. However, pedestrians felt the pressure wave on their ear drums while whipping hair and hoods in the whistling hiss of their passing. Still, response times were awful for almost every engagement.

Then, closer to the scene, chirping sirens in the darkness drowned out the crowd's muffled chanting and lamenting two blocks distant. Add the lightning-littered sky and this night would soon become one great gallery of dashed dreams with a thousand black and blue flickers.

The overwhelming peppery scent of wasabi on steroids permeated and perverted the already-thin air—an astringent that scoured sensitive and healthy lungs alike. Red, orange and blue strobes showered unseen innocents just below with stroboscopic dread. Routine debilitating fear would not loosen its intractable grip on most pedestrians tonight—those with any common sense, that is.

The bad guys were winning. Not just tonight, and not just here.

Yet this was an otherwise tolerable stormy evening, as long as you wore a mask and protection, except for the stench from the lake. This assumed you were foolish enough to walk in the open after dark. Especially if you still headed south on North Lakeshore Drive in the once-fashionable neighborhood they called the Near North Side a century ago.

Adjacent to the abandoned Navy Pier Park, protesters stumbled or back-pedaled. Some crawled. Greasy purple stains of riot gas residue splattered or soaked their skin and clothes like watery mucous. You could see some were stained with spatters of black in the dim surroundings that turned red in brighter light.

Most choked down their pain—less from their external wounds, more from gas residue entering and burning soft nasal and throat tissue. Some made their way, aided by comrades-in-arms. Some were blinded, stumbled over swirling trash or still-smoking cylindrical neon-yellow canisters marked *Riot Dye*.

And if you foolishly hadn't beaten a hasty retreat after witnessing all of this, an apathetic breeze transported billowing smoke from a block away to scrape your eyes. Your nostrils and throat swelled shut. Drawing breath became difficult if not improbable. Breathing was hard enough without all this fanfare.

Some cursed the invasive stench of concentrated wasabi that sucked the already near-toxic air from their lungs, accompanied by noses flowing like waterfalls inside their masks.

Riot die. Unmistakable. Unforgettable. Some thought unforgivable.

If you were *still* not deterred, venturing yet another block farther south this night meant taking your life in your hands. You would approach the bitter core of the maelstrom, of what began as a peaceful gathering proclaiming its dissatisfaction over social issues aplenty. Take your pick in the sea of unrest.

Exercising the unforgettable artifact of one's first

amendment rights tonight, or most nights, was dangerous, maybe even lethal. Sometimes these peaceful gatherings turned ugly. Like tonight. Often, the reasons weren't clear. Neither your eyes and ears nor spotty media coverage could be trusted. Politics, policy enforcement and citizenship marinated in the toxic stew of prolonged anger. It had all become just too confusing, a poison to the soul. Who now retaliated against whom? Most had lost track.

Only one of every ten calls for policy enforcement assistance received timely attention. The level of unrest in recent months had escalated to unimaginable proportions.

Too many nefarious agents trolled emergency services, flooding them with false alarms. Regardless, CED and CFD fielded a response to every voxcon—in time. At least so said the local and Alliance-wide feeds.

In this respect, Chicago did not differ from every other major Westican city. Especially the mammoth regionplexes that sprawled: incorporating, gobbling up contiguous burgs, towns and cities. As if these giant gatherings of humanity huddled together could offer safety.

Commuters in high-speed magnetic levitation transports—for anyone who could afford a private transport or locate a public train—made such population centers workable, at least for the affluent patricians.

Most mag-lev transports and trains still worked—unlike the vast majority of other public works—for those few who still commuted to jobs, about the only compelling motivation for venturing out. That, and groceries, when available. And liquor. Or to protest a plethora of perennial injustices.

Many stayed home to stay safe, especially the poverty-stricken plebeians. Or even to starve. Hard choices.

Inconvenient

Old Chicago, Williana

Neither Zaya French or his wife Sierra Blade had ventured to the surface in months.

With good reason.

Air quality in all the regionplexes harrowed even healthy lungs. All withered without help to breathe. And that said nothing of the invisible but invasive rays that pierced everyone and everything without shielding.

Chicago proper hugged the southern shores of a once-great lake that had grown so polluted and clotted it was unnavigable. And it offended anyone with a working nose. At least Chicago found some relief from the absence of huddled masses to their north.

You dared not catch another person's eye on the street. Passing within six feet of anyone could prove fatal for the few that wandered the streets anymore. There was hardly a single block that didn't feature its own dumpster fire or its remains. These smelly affairs had become more common than burglar bars on store windows—that is, on those not already boarded up. Most shop owners taped their windows' holes and cracks from the inside with plastisteel tape, or just shuttered their windows with solid panels—at least those who had the funds to do so.

As Zaya tried to explain their shopping mission to his young bride, she interrupted, "What on Earth is a cash register? And nothing about this place spells *convenience!*" Sierra Blade spotted the faded sign hanging askew, somewhat obscured by the building's peeling facade as they approached the small store's portal. She looked like a jittery urban warrior with a blustery but endearing attitude.

Sierra's husband—Zaya French—was ever the avid historian. A hundred years ago, that portal would have been propped open during the summer to invite in the late-afternoon lake breeze. Not anymore. Their eyes watered from the noxious vapors emanating from the lake.

Like every other inhabited structure these days, they couldn't afford to allow manicured air to escape. Or more likely in such bottom-tier establishments, like *Manny's Stop-n-Drop,* to prevent the stench drifting into the store.

Their masks stayed in place to deliver a slow O2 trickle. Cheap little convenience stores like this couldn't afford to supplement the stale, thin-air interior with an oxygen blend. Only the small operator's cube at the back of the store was so treated. An operator incapacitated by hypoxia was of no use to anyone.

Zaya smiled at Sierra hunched behind her mask, under her cowled hood lined with shielding, and behind her omnipresent goggles. She moved like some long-extinct jungle cat trying to hide the impression she was on the hunt. Her eyes never ceased darting about as if trouble lurked everywhere. Neither did Zaya's, but his more practiced demeanor made it seem natural.

They'd soon need to live off the land, as some used to say. For the past fifteen years, Sierra had grown all her own food in her own biodiverse soil. She bartered with their neighbors in The Digs beneath Old Chicago for other essentials. But they'd be leaving all that behind. As capable as she was, she was an alien up here, poor thing. At least Zaya had lived and worked topside as a journalist and podcaster for decades before meeting Sierra in 2150. His profession had often called for vigorous self-defense.

Zaya recalled how different the year 2163 was from just a few decades earlier, before Sierra's birth thirty years ago. Politics and pollution and pandemics drove change. Even a few good ones. He caught her staring at him as he held the door for her. She was nodding, as if agreeing with him. He had yet to verbalized his recollections. She did *that thing* again. He'd never take that for granted.

She has no idea what life is like for more than a few hours outside her precious Digs.

"I'll learn, sweetheart."

"Babe, you know poking around in my memories doesn't come without risk." He grinned at the love of his life, she as tall as he. Taller when she wasn't slouching so she wouldn't tower over her man. "And hey, I'm secure enough to love a taller woman." That crooked smirk always served him well. He loved that she slouched for him, but it was so unnecessary.

To gaze into those pools of cool green wonder—her inquisitive eyes through those iridescent lenses—also entailed the risk of losing focus. Up here, they both needed to stay sharp.

She acquired answers to her myriad questions with no more spoken words between either of them. Then, as she pecked at another of his more distant memories, he could hear disgust rise in her voice like a musical crescendo of exaggerated astonishment. A bitter bile rose in her throat. Her mask hid the compound effect of the disgusting revelation sculpting her face. "Cash? Really! Oh, now *that* is *profoundly* disturbing."

"Yeah, babe. They say ninety percent of all cash back in the day was so contaminated, they identified it as a fundamental carrier of global pandemics. Secondary only to viral infections spread by the human breath, by the way. Might have been less offensive to pay for groceries with soiled toilet paper."

"Toilet paper?"

"Never mind. But after most banks and credit companies collapsed, folks who had stashed cash used it to buy essentials. The twenties and thirties were scary times."

"Z, I've read the stories on the feeds."

For the first seventeen years of her life, Sierra lived with her mother, a corrupt power-hungry politician sent to the Cuban Penal Colony for the rest of her life. In the thirteen years since, Sierra voxconned her mother each month until she passed away two years ago—at the height of their relationship. That Libby Blade survived eleven years in the CPC was remarkable. But then, she had been a remarkable woman, if not misguided on a grand scale.

Alarms sounded and the turnstile barrier refused Sierra's entrance ahead of Zaya. She looked up and around. "What the... ?" Spoken by an indignant stranger in a strange land. The store's biometrics were frustrated by Sierra's mask, hood, goggles, and gloves, not to mention her goth-grunge olive-drab tunic, tactical belt and boots. She remained a mystery to the system responsible for identifying and qualifying customers for potential purchases.

Even without headwear and gloves, though, she wouldn't be bio-mapped in any database. The store could not identify her. Not even a voice or an ocular match. To this allegedly infallible but aging piece of infrastructure, she was nothing but an angry vapor. Thanks to friends of friends in high places at one time, and the passage of time underground, she did not exist.

Not mapped, no purchase. Period.

Zaya offered a congenial wave to the skeptical lady in her air-enhanced cube at the far end of the narrow but deep convenience store. Raised his right arm with an index finger pointing downward in a circular motion to flag the two of them as a couple.

The sensors had mapped him in a millisecond, so the store operator released the turnstile lock and Sierra pushed through against her better judgment. Zaya patted her on the shoulder from behind to ease her escalating anxiety.

She averted her gaze from the overhead lights. Zaya knew why. Through her goggles, only *she* could *see* the spurious emissions radiating from those cheap rectangular bulbs, not to mention the high-powered electromagnetic rays bolting every which way. Everywhere.

Now *Zaya's* level of concern escalated. "Babe, we gotta get you more comfortable with this stuff. You know that, right? B-man needs our help."

"I know. Let's do this." Her jittery jazz hands signaled this was not routine for her. Every camera in the place tracked her every gesture, her every suspicious movement. If cams had nerves....

Zaya selected a few items with little check mark waves of his right index finger near the store's proximity panel next to the menu description of each item he wished to purchase. A conveyor delivered their purchased items and plopped them into the fiber bag they'd brought with them.

Birdman's daughter Cherry made that bag for them, just for this safari. The last item jammed in the conveyor's jaws. He tugged it free and it dropped into their bag. More suspicious behavior.

Zaya remembered when delivery services still operated, but even then, they couldn't have located their low-profile refuge—a near-mythical subterranean labyrinth to outsiders. Few even knew of The Digs' existence. By intent. They grew food in their own nurtured soil, mined their own water and enjoyed a rich oxygen blend harvested from their lower-tunnel mini-farms with a distillation process of Sierra's invention. Everyone contributed, everyone benefited. Unlike topside.

"Can we go now, Z? Please? The noise... I'm... It's just too much for one day, okay? I'll do better another day. I promise."

Clenching and unclenching her fists garnered more unwanted attention than they deserved. They were on the verge of being auto-detained, so they beat a hasty departure after the prox panel debited his purchases on his implant.

With a curt nod to the store operator, they wheeled on their heels. Zaya projected a stiff right arm out front as if he were running interference. Pushed open the door. In his artificial left hand dangled the small half-full bag of items with the few essential items not available in The Digs. To Sierra's great relief, they headed for their sanctuary.

He needed to get her below before something bad happened.

Gentleman's Spy

New Wash, Maryginia

Before Edmond Blake became a career executive at the UWT Alliance Intelligence Agency, he distinguished himself as Eddy Blake—one of their finest investigators and intel aggregators. The AIA knew no finer spy-slash-cop. He even looked like the mythical James Bond of legend, but older, taller, broader and more severe. Since he'd jettisoned his few extra pounds, he looked like a cross between two of the old-time celebrities who played Bond in retro vids—Sean Connery crossed with Daniel Craig, but with an ivy league accent instead of a Scottish brogue—that was Edmond Blake. There was something else, but what? Boyish charm? A lethal kindness? Undeserved humility?

The case that earned him his elite agency's second-highest office—that of Executive Director of Operations—broke during his tenure as Executive Special Agent in Charge at the Alliance's largest field office in Chicago.

Though that tenure spanned less than three years, as ESAIC—pronounced "E-sake"—he grew to love that city, even though several assignments abroad earlier in his career also held special places in his eidetic memory.

In 2150 he broke the Grandy conspiracy in Chicago that would have otherwise decimated the planet's magnetosphere with apocalyptic implications. That singular case provided him notoriety sufficient to penetrate the fragile New Wash political ionosphere at AIA Headquarters after twenty-two years of exemplary service to the agency, and to the Westican people.

In short, solving that case earned him this desk.

For that definitive break, he owed an inestimable debt of gratitude and loyalty to CED Captain Judge Miners, now that mammoth city's policy enforcement commissioner. And to Detective Lionel Smith, now CED's chief of detectives. Plus, how could he forget that incorrigible rogue reporter and podcaster, Zaya French? Edmond would never forget that trio and their little entourage, especially that telepathic ex-priest, Lamatte Foliére, with whom he shared a certain... skill.

Edmond thought often, and with fondness, of the stunning Judge, pudgy Smitty, feisty Zaya, and cerebral Lamatte. He had not seen that meddlesome foursome for years, although he'd voxconned *her* at least quarterly. They all still lived in Chicago—ground zero.

He worried for their safety, maybe something else too, if he were honest with himself. He worried most about Commissioner Judge Miners. But they were both busy professionals with no time for personal lives.

Or are we?

Edmond looked around his new office. *Nobody* needed raised paneling of actual wood to adorn a space the size of a small ballroom, much less decorated with artwork that would feed hundreds of families for a year. *What a waste.* He clenched his lips, puckering his cheeks in subdued guilt at the flagrant opulence. *And this obscene desk! The monstrosity must weight at least two metric tons.*

Edmond dwelled on the misery from which so many Westicans suffered every day. Sixty percent lived on wages that peered *up* at poverty level, absent of any hope for their future. Eighty percent of all children under the age of ten went to bed hungry every single night. In *his* Westica! And if the color of your skin was anything other than white, well, despite the deniers, all bets were off, especially after dark.

The Alliance's infrastructure languished past the point of crumbling. Maybe in part because just three Westican trillionaires commanded more wealth than nine hundred million less-connected citizens not prepossessed of bulging off-planet accounts. His Alliance had gone to shit. *That explains the odor.*

People had been taking to the streets for decades with a dogged determination to exercise one of their few remaining rights still guaranteed by the Alliance's constitution, despite its nonstop re-codification. They clung to their right to peacefully assemble and to speak their minds even though they were being attacked with unprovoked brutality for exercising those rights. Now they were retaliating. En masse. They claimed their beloved constitution was now nothing more than an ancient piece of digital parchment on the verge of cracking into insignificant scraps from brittle corruption by the patrician class. *What a powder keg. This could consume our beloved Alliance if we don't do something.*

Over the last few days, his agency discovered troubling chatter. Chicago had become the Alliance's ground zero for anti-federal sentiment. Half of the city protested against neutered or squabbling Alliance leadership who did nothing for them, other than tax them. And the other half found itself pock-marked with starvation and street riots—pungent cesspools of violence instigated by opportunistic criminals.

The worst? An army of agitators—a lot of them—in the various communal feeds, once called social media, flooded policy enforcement with false calls, among other cyber violations. The common term for such criminals was *trolls*. They spanned the spectrum, so nobody knew what information to trust. Edmond saw *this* as the primary battlefield, with every vocal citizen or official now an ill-informed combatant or victim.

How on Earth have we come to this?

Now he watched his agency's budget and influence tumble toward obscurity. The current administration's tenure was merely a capstone to the ineffectiveness of a dozen previous administrations. The skirmish that raged in the pit of his stomach these days demanded... what? *Something must change.*

His boss was about to be fired by the Department of Judgment for inaction—in other words, disloyalty. Since Edmond flew below the radar, as they used to say back in the day when they still used that now-antiquated technology, they'd likely appoint him as acting director. The last mutt standing. Perhaps *that* would be his window of providence. In the meantime, he'd offer his friends a low-key assist, even though it might cost him the directorship.

"Commissioner Miners! I always look forward to hearing your voice." And he meant it.

Judge Miners huddled in her lush but cluttered office at 22 Policy Plaza deep within the heart of Chicago. She could ill-afford the time, but it was *him.* A friend in high places.

"EDO Blake, this is an honor. Haven't heard from you in months, although I see you on the Alliance-wide feeds. Seems you are a rising star. But to be blunt, why the voxcon now?"

"Ha! Well, to be equally blunt, your creative assist during that Grandy affair gave my career a timely boost, and I still owe you an immense debt of gratitude. It's time I offered you something in return, other than the occasional titillating repartee. I'm worried about your city. How can I help?"

"Honestly? The contingent of Alliance agents the administration sent here to *help* causes far more problems than it solves. To be clear, neither the governor, the mayor, nor I invited that alleged assistance. They only know how to escalate already incendiary situations. They're soldiers, not peacekeepers. Not their fault. That's their training. Can you get someone to call them off, Edmond?"

"I thought it might be something like that. I'll see what I can do. And I thank you for your candor."

A five second pause announced the conversation had run its intended course. Then Blake addressed her in an unexpectedly personal tone, using her unusual first name.

"Judge, how *are* you? It seems your plate overflows."

"Yes, Edmond. We're managing. But all these troops, all that armament, their bullying tactics, and their illegal seizures make our job harder, not easier. It's universally pissing off everyone here, including civilians in the streets. I appreciate your offer to help with that. So to your question, I'm managing. How are *you* faring inside the New Wash beltway?"

His response seemed only to offer cursory reciprocity in response to her refreshing candor, but veered toward boilerplate. So obvious—outside his comfort zone. Blake cut the call short.

Another pressing matter, he said.

Miners wondered if anyone outside her own small circle of confidantes knew of Edmond's remarkable telepathic abilities, so rare in his circles. Most of those folks head for the hills (or the tunnels).

She also wondered if he sensed the electric thrill that jangled her whenever she heard his voice. Both of them chalked up their quarterly tête-à-têtes to *networking,* a straightforward liaison between municipal and Alliance officials. But recently, something changed. Edmond had taken a tremendous political risk by offering to help her troubled city. Why? Was it all business? Or something else?

WHAT'S NEXT?

If you like what you've seen of *"Mayhem: Mean Streets,"*
please go to
GKJurrens.com
or purchase a copy from your favorite online retailer.
Available in paperback and eBook editions.

OTHER BOOKS BY GK JURRENS

Contemporary Fiction (Adventure)

- Dangerous Dreams: Dream Runners: Book 1
- Fractured Dreams: Dream Runners: Book 2

Historical Fiction (Great Depression Era Crime)

- Black Blizzard: A Lyon County Adventure
- Murder in Purgatory: A Lyon County Mystery

Futuristic Fiction (Paranormal Mystery Thrillers)

- Underground, Mayhem: Book 1
- Mean Streets, Mayhem: Book 2
- Post Earth, Mayhem: Book 3
- A Glimpse of Mayhem: Companion Guide to the Mayhem Trilogy

Non-fiction

- Why Write? Why Publish? Passion? Profit? Both?
- Moving a Boat and Her Crew
- Restoring a Boat and Her Crew

BEFORE YOU GO

Please write and post a brief review online where you bought this book. Or email your thoughts to gjurrens@yahoo.com. Remember, other readers and I need to know what you think. **I read every single review with gratitude.**
Thank you.
Also, feel free to browse or subscribe at GKJurrens.com for announcements and giveaways.

- GK Jurrens

ABOUT THE AUTHOR

GK Jurrens writes with undiluted passion.

He also teaches writing and publishing on the road. Most of the time, GK and his wife live and travel in a motorhome when they're not spending time at their condo in Southwest Florida. They find wandering their beloved North America a source of endless inspiration.

After four years of government service (plus two more in the Reserves), GK earned several degrees while mounting a successful three-decade career in high technology.

Now he spends as much time as possible with his partner Kay. GK practices Yoga and Transcendental Meditation, writes, paints, and plays Native American-style flutes, some of which he handcrafted while living in the Arizona desert. He also studies the Japanese Shakuhachi flute, arguably one of the most difficult instruments to play well.

GK's favorite quote: ***"The difference between ordeal and adventure is attitude!"***

Follow GK (Gene) on:

amazon.com/author/gkjurrens
goodreads.com/gkjurrens
twitter.com/gjurrens1
facebook.com/genejurrens

www.ingramcontent.com/pod-product-compliance
Lightning Source LLC
Chambersburg PA
CBHW030350200726
48286CB00013B/764